BLOOD RAIN

A SHADOW DETECTIVE NOVEL

WILLIAM MASSA

CRITICAL MASS PUBLISHING

Copyright © 2017 by WILLIAM MASSA

All rights reserved.

No part of this book may be reproduced in any form or by any electronic or mechanical means, including information storage and retrieval systems, without written permission from the author, except for the use of brief quotations in a book review.

1

"What have you done?"

The ominous question hung in the loft like a dark cloud, the accusatory tone in Skulick's voice unmistakable.

"I-I had to save her..." I stammered. "She was dying. I had no choice." My words felt weak and half-hearted, a guilty man lacking the confidence to defend his own actions.

Talk about royally screwing up. A misguided attempt to save the woman I love had doomed her to an undead state. What possessed me to grab the chalice and pour its thick, scarlet liquid down Jane Archer's throat? How could I have been so foolish?

The answer was simple. Desperation is the mother of all bad decisions.

Our headquarters held some of the most powerful

magical artifacts known to mankind. Skulick and my father had confiscated many of them when I was still stumbling around in diapers. Even though we'd been working together for more than three years now, my partner was notoriously secretive about these occult relics, feeling the less I knew about them, the safer I'd be. The origins of the golden, rune-engraved chalice had been just one of the vault's many secrets.

Locking up magical artifacts didn't rob them of their black magic. The dark power contained within these accursed items yearned to be free. Yearned to inflict maximum carnage upon the world. The relics spoke to us every time we entered the vault, each one seductive in its own way, an all-too-persuasive choir of evil. I thought I'd trained myself to ignore them, yet I'd fallen under the chalice's unholy spell.

I can heal your woman, the relic had whispered. *I can save her...*

God, I should've known better than to step into the vault when I was at my most vulnerable. The chalice had taken advantage of my own weakness—but that didn't excuse what I'd done. Understanding that forces beyond my control had manipulated me didn't change the terrible reality of what we now faced. I had unleashed a new monster upon the city, a beast determined to prey on the living.

A shrill cry cut through the night, reverberating eerily.

I swallowed hard as my gaze turned toward the shattered window through which Archer had escaped. Our base was protected by both electronic security measures as well as magical wards, but the protective runes only worked one way. They kept the monsters out but had failed to keep Archer in. The hair on the back of my neck prickled as the screams outside intensified. Archer must've found her first victim.

I had to go after her. Stop her before it was too late and innocents were hurt. Every life she took in her transformed state would weigh on my conscience. More than that, Archer wouldn't have wanted to live like this. I refused to let her pay the price for my foolishness.

Brushing past a still glaring Skulick, *Hellseeker* out and ready, I tore into the elevator. Reaching the ground floor seemed to take forever. My impatience boiling over, I burst out of the lift as soon as it came to a standstill.

I needed to find Archer before she killed someone.

I prayed I wouldn't be too late.

Cold rain lashed my face as I emerged from the warehouse, wind buffeted my soaking wet coat. I didn't expect the rain to cease any time soon. Even though Skulick and I had successfully prevented the Crimson Circle from unleashing Hell on Earth a year ago, they'd still managed to breach the veil that separated our world from the dimension of darkness. This weakening of the barrier had led a sharp uptick in paranormal activity—and some of the worst weather conditions the city had ever endured. No wonder we'd nicknamed the sprawling metropolis the 'Cursed City.' If having to contend with ghouls and demons wasn't enough, the sun was usually hidden behind heavy, black storm clouds these days. This lack of sunlight could wear on anyone's mental wellbeing.

And everyone knows that monsters come out to play in the dark.

Ignoring the sting of the icy rain, I pressed onward. I didn't have to go far before I stumbled upon Archer's first victim.

My roaming gaze landed on a homeless man, his eyes wide and glassy with burgeoning madness. Blood oozed from his throat, his ratty, dirt-caked coat soaked red. The downpour had failed to wash away the evidence of the vicious vampire attack.

There was no sign of Archer.

My heart quickened, secretly glad she'd vanished. The idea of having to unload *Hellseeker* into my love made me sick to my stomach. But what other choice would I have once our paths crossed again? There was no other way to stop a vampire.

I grabbed the terrified man's shoulders. "Where did the woman go?"

I refused to call Archer a vampire to the man's face.

The bleeding fellow stared at me blankly, his mind having checked out long before he ran into a blood starved monster in a rainy alley. Our loft was located in the gritty outskirts of the city, surrounded by derelict alleys, abandoned warehouses, and the tented cities of the lost who dwelled on the fringes of society. There would be no witnesses to point me in the right direction, no patrol cars that might encounter Archer and try to pick her up. On the positive side, this reduced the chances of further collateral damage.

I checked the man's wounds. Despite the large amount of blood, he didn't seem to be in immediate danger. I drew some comfort from the fact that Archer had attacked the man without resorting to lethal force. Hopefully it signaled that still some small part of her true self remained intact.

Maybe I can still save her...

Who was I kidding? Maybe the old Archer was still in charge, but the black blood roaring through her veins would sweep away the last traces of her humanity soon enough. I'd infected her with the curse of the vampire. There was no coming back from that.

Hollywood had gotten many of the details about these mythical monsters wrong over the years. For example, crosses were utterly useless against vampires unless imbued with magical properties. But one of the poplar myths did hit close to the truth. To turn a human, vampires needed to completely drain their victims and feed them their unholy blood. Archer had merely taken a sip from the old man.

Reassured that he wouldn't bleed out on the street, I continued down the dumpster-lined alley. Rain drummed rhythmically against rusting metal containers overflowing with trash, producing a hypnotic beat. It all felt like a bad dream. But there would be no awakening from this nightmare, no reprieve from my guilt.

Incoming sirens suddenly bashed the night. I whirled toward the fast-approaching headlights as they speared the rainy darkness around me. Tires screeched and sent plumes of rainwater my way. With everything else going on, I'd forgotten that the Cursed City's finest believed that I had abducted—and quite possibly murdered—two of their detectives. To be fair, they were right. But one of them had been a serial killer, and Archer...well, I had no excuse for what I'd done to her.

The cops flung the cruiser's doors open, and the uniformed officers emerged, guns up, voices barking. Within seconds, they slammed me against the wet hood of the cruiser. It certainly didn't help that the homeless man's blood covered my shirt and flecked my beard.

Metal bit into my skin as one of the brawny cops snapped a pair of cuffs on me. The boys in blue unceremoniously pushed me into the back of the patrol car. From what seemed like a great distance, I could hear one of the cop's reading me my rights without much enthusiasm. My wrists hurt, but I welcomed the pain.

I deserved what was coming to me. And then some.

I lost all sense of time as we drove through the city, rain *pitter-pattering* on the roof. Less than an hour later, I found myself at some gritty, noisy precinct, facing down two homicide detectives inside a stuffy interrogation room. I identified myself, informed the officers that I served as a special consultant who helped the police with occult cases, and requested to see Detective Benson, my liaison with the force.

Then I clammed up.

The detectives backed off and left me alone in the tiny interrogation room. The stale air reeked of sour sweat of desperate criminals. I sat slumped forward in the chair, a bloody, tattered, rain-soaked shadow of my former self.

I don't know how much time passed before Detective Benson joined me in my cell of misery. The tall African-American homicide detective couldn't quite hide the shock at seeing me in my current condition. His neatly pressed suit stood in sharp contrast to my ragged, rumpled state. He took a seat in front of me, his eyes searching my face.

Benson was used to dealing with the dark side of humanity. But there were things out there far worse than the most deranged murderers. Much worse. That's when he usually called me. But despite our working relationship, Benson had never totally trusted me. Now whatever goodwill there'd been between us was evaporating fast. He looked at me the way a cop looks at a criminal.

"Where are Detective Archer and Detective Lucas?" he asked.

"They're gone," I whispered.

His eyes widened ever so slightly and he said, "Are you telling me they're dead?"

I could only shrug.

"Damn it, Raven! Talk to me!"

The dam holding my swirling emotions tightly in check broke and the words started to pour out of me. It was confession time. I told him about what happened at Blackwell Penitentiary, about the horrors we had encountered in the abandoned prison and how one of his own detectives revealed himself to be the infamous serial killer *Lucifer's Disciple* before turning on me and Archer. My voice shook, dropping half an octave, when I came to the part where Archer died.

"You have to understand, I was not thinking straight" I said, choked with emotion. "I did it to save her. There was no other way..."

"What in God's name did you do to her, Raven?"

I remained silent. Benson's eyes popped, his impatience detonating. "Talk to me, goddamnit! What did you do to Detective Archer?"

I damned the woman I love, I thought grimly.

Damned us both to Hell.

2

The punch landed with the force of a sledgehammer, whipping my head back, a long strand of scarlet saliva exploding from my lips.

I stumbled back a few feet, barely able to maintain my balance. Copper filled my mouth, and I spit blood. My tongue flicked across my teeth, making sure they were still all there. The world tilted, and I narrowed my eyes, struggling to regain my bearings.

The massive, blurry creature in front of me snapped back into focus. This was no monster from the deepest pits of Hell though, but merely some beefcake who spent way too much of his leisure time trying to give the Rock a run for his money. Tattoos lined every square inch of the bald meathead's bulging arms. Not exactly the kind of guy you'd want to be fighting in some trash-infested back alley, even if said alley was located behind your favorite dive bar.

The bastard outweighed me by at least fifty pounds, and the first couple of punches hadn't been due to luck. He pressed his lips into a mean slash, his eyes shiny with bloodlust.

How had I gotten myself into this latest pickle?

Nearly a month had passed since I faced down Benson back at the precinct. I wish I could say the weeks following Archer's transformation into a vampire had been productive. Instead of making any progress in finding her or discovering a cure for vampirism, I'd embarked on a vicious, self-destructive downward spiral of boozing and feeling sorry for myself, interspersed with random acts of violence.

Normally "acts of violence" were code for chasing after some nightmare creature, but paranormal activity was at an all-time low. My odds of getting into some sort of alcohol-fueled bar scrape were higher nowadays than running into some supernatural beast of prey. Maybe it was my rundown state, or the stench of booze oozing off me, but I was developing a talent for pushing the wrong buttons in the wrong kinds of a-holes.

Case in point: Thor, Jr., who had zero intention of letting me leave this alley in one piece. He'd been harassing a lovely biker babe all night long until I couldn't take it anymore and stepped in. I'd been looking forward to a mind numbing evening of drinking. Unfortunately, the universe had other plans for me, and that's how I found myself sobering up in a freezing cold alley with a tattooed meathead as my dancing partner.

I'd almost welcomed this violent break from my self-pity party. At least until the first punch landed, and I spit up my last couple of drinks.

What a waste, I thought dimly as I retched.

Three more punches connected. A dirty grin lit up the biker's meaty visage. Our one-sided bout was clearly therapeutic for both of us, albeit in different ways. Despite my recent self-destructive tendencies, I was starting to get pissed. Anger outweighing self-pity, I managed to block the next three blows while landing two punches of my own.

That's right, dude. Don't mess with me. I hunt monsters for a living.

The biker stumbled, savagery giving way to surprised disappointment. His bros took a few steps back, finely tuned street instincts sensing that this brawl might play out differently than expected.

Unwilling to accept he might be up against someone who knew how to handle himself even with one too many drinks in their system, biker boy lunged at me.

I expertly snatched one of his meaty arms, using his momentum against him with martial arts grace as I hurtled his bulk over my shoulder. Skulick had taught me every dirty fighting trick in the book and a few that had never been written down. For more than a decade, a morning sparring session with my partner had been part of my daily workout regimen, and it had turned me into a fighter of considerable skill.

Or at least it did when I was sober. In my current drunken state, my reaction time had become a joke. Skulick would've easily knocked me on my ass, despite the wheelchair. But I was still skilled enough to teach this asshole a lesson.

The bastard landed on his back with a loud *whoomp*, the impact driving the air out his lungs. Before he could react, I grabbed his arm again, yanked it upward, and twisted the outstretched limb sharply. There was a sick crunch, and he let out a decidedly un-macho shriek of pain.

His crew retreated further as I whirled toward them, a savage grin plastered on my face. Clearly there wasn't much loyalty between these scumbags because nobody made even a token effort to help the fallen biker. I loomed over my attacker like some blood-stained madman, raised my fist, and inhaled sharply. What the hell was I doing? Was I really going to beat some stupid bar rat into a pulp just to make myself feel better?

I was taking out my rage on this fool when I should be looking for Archer. But how do you track someone when they seemed to have vanished off the surface of the Earth? Newly made vampires were voracious beasts, more animal than human, unable to control their need for blood.

Archer should have left a trail of dead bodies in her wake, but none of the newsfeeds and police bands Skulick monitored with near religious intensity suggested a brand-new vampire was on the loose.

Older vampires were closer to the ones in the movies. And when I say older, I'm talking centuries. After a few hundred years, their inhuman cravings became more manageable, allowing vampires to blend in with human society to a degree. Younger vamps were a whole other story and shared more in common with ravenous zombies—way more *Walking Dead* than *Twilight,* if you catch my drift. So what was going on here? Even if Archer was targeting homeless people, the most vulnerable targets on our tough city streets, the cops should be stumbling across the bodies by now.

I didn't want to confront the thing Archer had become, but not knowing where she was felt even worse. I had created this mess and I needed to resolve it, the sooner the better. In our business, no news wasn't good news but an indicator that a real shitstorm was about to hit.

I wiped the blood from my face and walked—okay, limped—out of the alley without a word. I might've defeated Biker Boy, but not before he managed to land some solid blows. The right side of my face was puffing up and my upper body throbbed. The bruises would keep me company for a few days, the pain a reminder of the lesson I'd learned tonight: When the guilt from turning your would-be girlfriend into a vampire threatens to tear you apart, don't take it out on strangers.

Despite my condition, I located the Equus Bass, my jet-black, ward-protected muscle car that would have made Mad Max envious, and slipped behind the wheel. I tried to not get any blood on the leather upholstery but failed miserably. Too drunk to drive, I decided to wait it out. I leaned back, and before I knew it, I was out cold. The next thing I remember was some guy flashing me a shit-eating grin as he took a piss against a nearby fire hydrant.

Talk about a lovely sight to wake up to.

I felt like someone had cracked my skull and patched it back together with a rusty stapler. My gut wrenched as I snapped open the glove compartment, extricating three Advils which I washed down with a thermos of stale coffee. Breakfast of champions.

Ten minutes later, I finally felt coherent enough to start the car and make my way back to the converted warehouse I shared with Skulick. It served as both our quarters and base of operations, and over time the loft had begun to feel like home. On the way, I stopped off at a local taco truck and helped myself to the greasiest breakfast burrito on the menu—and possibly the planet. My stomach lurched and threatened to revolt, but I knew that a grease bomb was my best shot at salvaging the day ahead.

I even ordered a second burrito for Skulick. See, I'm not a completely terrible human being.

The smell of fresh coffee quickened my pulse as I staggered into the loft. Skulick might be a lousy cook, but he sure as hell knew how to brew a mean cup of joe. My mentor downed the stuff by the gallons. He was already seated behind his vast bank of monitors, quashing any chance of slipping into my bedroom unnoticed.

Ever since a rampaging spirit had dropped Skulick out of a three-story window, he'd been stuck in a wheelchair. I sought refuge in the bottle when times got tough, but Skulick had his shit together. Instead of wallowing in self-pity, he had turned his setback into an asset. Every moment of his day was dedicated to monitoring the web and police bands for signs of supernatural activity. He truly was the Cursed City's guardian, looking over her with the devoted intensity of a samurai protecting his master.

And as for me? I was just the muscle, an enforcer with an enchanted gun. At least that's what it felt like these days.

My relationship with Skulick had been strained since the incident with Archer, and we hadn't been talking much lately. And on the rare occasions when we did exchange words...well, let's just say that I had entered the "anger" stage of grief. I kept asking him why he'd kept a cup filled with highly infectious vampire blood in our vault, but he'd remained mum on the manner.

I'd always believed that only a live vampire could make more of its kind, but obviously Skulick had known more than he'd let on. Somehow the grail possessed magical properties which had preserved the vampire blood's power to infect the living.

I suspected that the grail and the blood might be connected to the vampire attack that had set Skulick on his monster hunting path nearly thirty years earlier. My partner hadn't been exactly forthcoming about the details of that incident, either. All I knew was that Skulick, a homicide detective at the time, had been on the trail of a mysterious serial killer who had turned out to be a vampire. The vamp had transformed Skulick's fiancée into a creature of the night, which had understandably almost pushed him over the edge. Fortunately, my father had arrived, and together they hunted and defeated the vampire. In the wake of these events, Skulick had joined my father's monster-hunting quest.

The rest was history, as they say. Seeing my own love transformed into a creature of the night was stirring up old memories. Memories he would rather keep buried.

For a split second, I foolishly believed I could steal my way into my room without having to exchange any words with my mentor. Maybe he was so wrapped up in his work that he wouldn't notice me.

"You have another productive night of feeling sorry for yourself?"

The man might've lost his ability to walk, but he still had the ears of a bat.

I caught sight of my reflection in the window and realized what I must look like to Skulick. If reeking of alcohol wasn't bad enough, my face looked like someone had decided to try out a new Zumba dance routine on it.

Skulick spun around in his state-of-the art wheelchair. For a beat, he didn't say anything. Truth be told, he didn't have to. His eyes spoke volumes. Skulick wasn't just a partner; he was like a father to me. He'd raised me after my parents were murdered by demons. His palpable disappointment stung, and I lowered my face, suddenly ten years old again.

"How long do you plan to keep this up?"

"None of your business," I said. Yup, definitely feeling like a kid who'd gotten in trouble. In a minute, I'd say something like "You're not my real dad!" and storm off to my room.

"Everything you do is my business." His wheelchair inched closer. "I invested too much in you to see you throw it all away." He paused, his eyes fixed on me. "I know you're hurting, you lost someone who was...close to you."

"That's a nice way of putting it," I said. "I turned the woman I love into a goddamn monster."

Skulick clenched his jaw. "We've gone over this before," he said curtly. "You know all too well the powerful sway some of the relics can have. They plant seeds in our minds, wait for us to be at our most vulnerable."

"I don't need you to explain or make excuses--"

"Then I won't. You fucked up, kid. Big time. But it's time you put this behind you and focus on the challenges which lie ahead."

"Easy for you to say, old man."

His eyes narrowed as he scowled at me. "I'm tired of seeing you piss away everything we worked so hard for. We are at war, in case you'd forgotten. Our enemy has been quiet, but it's only a matter of time before the forces of darkness strike again. And we better be ready for them when they do."

I was considering another smartass comeback but caught myself. As usual, Skulick was right. Our mission was greater than any one of us. Like it or not, Skulick and I were the Cursed City's best defense in the ongoing battle with the darkness. My own personal demons paled in comparison with the literal ones that threatened our world. I reached for the steaming pot of coffee, and I poured myself a cup. The sizzling hot brew burned its way down my throat and made me feel human again. This was some powerful shit. Rocket fuel for the soul.

"How are things looking out there?" I asked after I'd drained most of the cup.

"No word on any vampire attacks but Detective Benson called just before you showed up looking like a recruiting poster for the local AA chapter."

I perked up. Benson hadn't contacted me since the events at Blackwell Penitentiary. If he was reaching out now, it meant the cops were dealing with a paranormal crime scene. It also suggested that Benson had decided I deserved a second chance to earn his trust.

"He sounded pretty freaked out on the phone," Skulick added. "Said he'd never seen anything like this before."

Now that was troubling. This wasn't Benson's first rodeo on the dark side. We'd worked on a series of supernatural cases over the last year that would have made any sane man look forward to retirement. When Benson sounded scared, Skulick paid attention. And so did I.

"I guess that shower will have to wait for a little while longer," I said, trying to be funny. Skulick refused to crack a smile. Tough room.

I leaned over the stainless-steel coffee pot and somehow managed to fill up my thermos without spilling a drop. Nice to know my hand-eye coordination remained intact even after a beating. I was just about to leave when Skulick's wheelchair swiveled toward me once more.

"One more thing," he began.

I tensed. "What else?"

"I hope you're not afraid of heights." Skulick eyed me for a beat and added, "That's what Benson told me to tell you."

I let that sink in for a beat, imagining all the scenarios in which such a phobia might be relevant for this latest case.

"What was your response?"

A grin played across my partner's features and he said, "I told him monster hunters weren't afraid of anything."

Now there was a lie if I ever heard one.

I feared the dark.

I feared the nightmares which lurked within it.

But most importantly, I feared losing the people I cared about.

3

I hope you're not afraid of heights.

As I stepped onto the roof of the seventy-story office tower, Benson's words were beginning to make a lot more sense. A yawning abyss of steel and cement greeted me. Wind buffeted my coat and tousled my hair. The Cursed City stretched out in every direction, a breathtaking sight from these great heights.

Instead of triggering a panic attack, the dizzying view reminded me of what it was all about. The urban sprawl was a living, breathing organism fueled by millions of lives; lives I'd sworn to protect from the forces of Hell. Whether the people below knew it or not, they trusted me to keep them safe. I'd forgotten that as I tried to drown my problems these last weeks.

I turned my attention away from the streets below. The rooftop had become a bustling crime scene. Everywhere I looked, I spotted CSI technicians and uniformed cops, the officers forced to hold on to their hats against the blistering wind.

As the crowd of cops parted, a body stood revealed at the center of the roof. Twisted limbs poked from beneath a blood-soaked sheet, the wind buffeting the edges of the shroud.

I swallowed hard. There were certain things one never quite got used to. Over the years, I'd visited some unusual crime scenes, but this rooftop murder was giving me a bad feeling in my gut.

As I gingerly approached the corpse, I overheard one of the detectives interviewing a uniformed building superintendent.

"Who else has keys to this area?" the detective inquired.

"Besides me? Nobody."

"And the roof access door was locked when you found the body?"

"Yes, sir."

The detective looked around, at a loss for a logical explanation. I felt bad for the guy; crime in the Cursed City had a way of defying standard investigative techniques. The normal rules of deductive reasoning rarely applied to the strange and gruesome crimes committed by the creatures of darkness.

Still, the detective did his best. "Well, is there another way out here?"

"Nope, just the one door," the superintended replied.

The detective was still trying to wrap his head around this information when my gaze found Detective Benson in the crowd. He acknowledged my presence but there was little warmth in the man's dark, hooded eyes.

I didn't blame Benson. After all, I'd turned his best detective into a vampire and set her loose on the city. In a way, it was nice to know I wasn't the only one who thought I screwed up royally. Nevertheless, Benson was a professional and refused to let personal feelings interfere with our working relationship.

He shielded his cigarette as he lit it and took a deep drag. Smoke swirling around his face, he sidled up to me and studied my battered features.

"What happened? You cut yourself shaving?"

I shot Benson a long look.

"Let me guess, a gang of leprechauns beat you up?"

Wow, someone was on a roll today.

"Leprechauns aren't real."

"Hard to keep track what's real and what's not these days. But thanks for clearing that up for me."

"I'm not some wizard cop chasing down the rejects of a *Lord of the Rings* casting call here. We're dealing with some evil shit."

"No kidding." The humor left Benson's eyes as he stole a quick glance at the shroud-covered body.

"So what do we know besides the fact that locked doors

don't seem to faze our killer and that he isn't afraid of heights?"

Benson took another drag from his cigarette and stomped the half-smoked butt under his heel. I thought he'd quit months ago, but working law enforcement in the Cursed City made it difficult to break bad habits—as I knew all too well from personal experience.

"The building superintendent found the body early this morning. Judging from the degree of lividity, I'd say our vic was killed around three or four a.m."

The Witching Hour, I thought. The time at which such creatures as witches, demons and ghosts were at their most powerful. Skulick had a couple of theories as to why it was such a popular time of night with the forces of darkness. There are no regular prayers or services in the Catholic Canonical hours between three and four. Some occult scholars claimed that the so-called Devil's Hour was an inversion of the time Christ died at Calvary.

It was all superstition and useless academic posturing, if you asked me. Monsters and demons didn't stick to arbitrary timetables dictated by the religions of the world. Their power went far beyond such belief systems. Nevertheless, homicidal occultists dabbling with forces beyond their control sometimes had a hard time differentiating fact from fiction and could well draw inspiration from such archaic notions.

"The building closes to the public after nine o'clock," I said, recalling the sign I'd passed on the door earlier.

Benson nodded.

"And the only people who would have been here were the building super and a couple of guards, right? None of whom are under that sheet?"

Another nod.

"So you're saying someone broke into this tower to dump a body?"

"It's a little more complicated than that. Security mans the downstairs lobbies and there are cameras on every floor. Guards saw nothing, and the cameras didn't fare much better. So far, reviewing the surveillance CCTV feed has produced zilch."

My eyes landed on the shroud-covered body. Only a few feet separated us now.

"Could the killer have tampered with the system?"

"Anything is possible. Either way, whoever is behind this, he's good. Better than good."

Benson had a point. Entering a high-security building and finding a way around both human and electronic security was no mean feat. There were quite a number of occult rituals that could bestow invisibility—if the person was willing make the necessary sacrifices. Or the killer could have conjured some supernatural entity to do the task for him or her.

I took in the crime scene. "This isn't just a murder. It's a statement. What better way to get the attention of this city than to turn one of its tallest buildings into a place of death?"

Benson nodded in agreement. "That's what I thought, too."

"Have you ID'd the victim yet?" I asked.

"Ronald Davison. He's one of the most successful attorneys in the city. Was, I should say. Not to speak ill of the dead, but he also happened to be a major scumbag."

My eyebrows turned upward. "The name sounds familiar."

"Davison tended to represent some of the worst folks this city has to deal with," Benson explained. "Drug dealers, mob members, celebrities who commit crimes. If you were rich and guilty, you'd call Davison and the bastard would do his best to mine every loop hole in the book to get you off."

I considered Benson's words. "Sounds like a real loss to society."

"Agreed. But we still have to figure who or what killed the bastard."

I shifted my attention to the nearest CSI tech. "You have a cause of death?"

The tech hesitated for a beat before he replied. "We do, but it doesn't quite add up."

What does these days? I thought and said, "I'm a pretty open-minded type of guy, so try me."

"Catastrophic injuries caused by what appears to have been an uncontrolled fall."

I frowned and motioned for him to go on.

"The way the body's crushed, the number of broken bones, the blood pattern, it all suggests a fall," the forensic tech explained. "A very high fall. At least a couple of hundred feet."

I mulled this latest revelation over. "So the killer dropped him off a cliff and then carted his body all the way up here?"

"Not exactly," the tech said. "See, based on the forensic evidence, the body's angle..."

"The victim was dropped on top of the roof," I finished.

"I know how it sounds, but--" The CSI tech broke off, at a loss for words.

I tilted my head toward the cloudy sky, the unforgiving wind making my eyes water. Something had dropped Davison on top of a skyscraper.

Benson eyed me expectantly. "You got anything for me, Raven? What kind of spooky shit is this?"

I shrugged. It was still too early to draw any conclusions.

In my line of work, I'd come across any number of monsters capable of taking to the air. Had some winged demonic beast hurled this man to his death?

I scanned my surroundings more carefully, my attention drawn to the four gargoyles that sprouted from the corners of the rooftop. Numerous rooftops sported these old protective symbols, but the detail on these stone beasts was impressive.

Maybe too impressive.

I approached the edge of the roof, my eyes landing on the ledge, searching for some sort of evidence that might explain the presence of the dead body. I wasn't convinced yet that this was a supernatural case. Maybe Davison had gone skydiving...without a parachute...over downtown. I shook my head at the silly thought. The case was weird but did it fit into my occult jurisdiction?

Benson appeared on my side, and to my surprise, he handed me a pair of binoculars. My eyebrows arched upward in a question, but I accepted the binoculars.

"Take a look," he urged me.

Still not sure what Benson was getting at, I followed his instructions. A series of nearby apartment buildings, most only half as tall as the Lenox Building, jumped into view. I swept the area, determined to figure out why Benson had handed the binos to me in the first place.

It felt like a test, or one of those Where's Waldo scenes. A variety of city dwellers were visible in the windows of their high-level apartments: a middle-aged man watching a daytime soap, a woman doing Zumba, a young college-aged kid nursing a smoothie on a balcony. One figure after another, a diverse cross section of the city's population.

"Bring the binoculars down a little bit."

"What am I supposed to be looking for here?" I asked at last, my voice laced with impatience.

"The victim's apartment."

Just as Benson uttered the words, I located the apartment unit in question. Peering through the binoculars, I could make out a shattered window on the tenth floor of the neighboring structure, a group of cops milling about on the unit's balcony.

I lowered the binoculars and peered down at the neighboring apartment building with my own eyes. It was located about fifteen city blocks from our crime scene.

"Nuts, huh?" Benson said.

I couldn't argue with the sentiment. Something had whisked the dead lawyer from his ten-story apartment building in an explosion of glass and lifted him through the air for eight city blocks before dropping him to his death right above this considerably taller rooftop.

A nerve twinged in the back of my neck as my focus turned back toward the massive gargoyle figures guarding the rooftop—silent witnesses to the crime, unable to divulge their secret knowledge. What would they tell me if they could speak? I'd never know, but I did know one thing for certain: this was beginning to look more and more like my kind of case.

4

I don't know how Benson pulls this stuff off, but he somehow managed to get me to the dead lawyer's building in less than thirty minutes despite rush hour traffic. Having a screaming siren on your unmarked police cruiser never hurts.

Arriving at the vic's apartment building, an all-too-familiar scene greeted me. Reporters struggled to put together a story while the cops did their best to keep the newshounds at bay. A tall, smartly dressed detective addressed the crowd, promising to answer their questions in an orderly fashion as long as everyone calmed down and shut up.

We fought our way past the throng and caught the next elevator. Benson stabbed the up-button, and the elevator hummed to life. Trying to break the uncomfortable silence between us, I said, "Did I ever tell you I hate elevators?"

Benson merely looked at me.

I took his silence as an invitation to continue. "When I was five, I got stuck in one. Scariest thing. Took them like five hours to get me out. Had nightmares for weeks--"

"Did you shower today?" Benson said, interrupting my trip down memory lane. "You smell like old booze."

Talk about a conversation stopper. Fortunately, the elevator dinged and the doors parted.

Without exchanging another word, we headed for the dead lawyer's apartment. Cops and forensic techs had taken over the luxurious four-bedroom unit that occupied half the floor. A jagged maw of glass framed a far-off view of the tall skyscraper where the lawyer's broken remains had been dumped. Benson led me onto the unit's bustling balcony. Once again, a dizzying perspective greeted me. Gusts of wind whipped my face. At this rate, I might develop a fear of heights.

I shifted my gaze upward as a police helicopter screamed by overhead and then spotted the reason why Benson had wanted me to inspect the balcony. A row of broken windows extended across a series of floors above Davison's unit, the side of the building streaked with a long trail of blood. Whatever aerial beast had snatched Davison, it had dragged him up along the apartment building before taking to the skies. For a moment, I could picture the hapless lawyer as he was carried off, arms flailing, hard cement scraping skin.

I took in the surreal sight and stepped back into the apartment. I'd seen enough.

As I walked through the luxurious dwelling, my eyes combing the place for anything of supernatural significance, one question kept going through my mind: Why Ronald Davison? Had he become a random victim or was he targeted by some dark force?

I decided to look around a bit more, see if anything might jump out at me. Each room in the spacious penthouse apartment was elegantly decorated, projecting a refined sensibility honed by a lucrative law practice. The eclectic mix of designer furniture and expensive art pieces suggested that Davison was either a man of taste or was smart enough to hire a talented interior designer.

I perused the framed degrees and awards on one wall, searching for any clue that might shed some light on the crime. Clearly Davison reveled in his accomplishments. I had to push past the surface and not allow myself to be blinded by the shiny razzle dazzle and bling of my surroundings.

It took me about ten minutes before I received my first hint that something might be rotten in Denmark. It was a subtle detail that would easily go unnoticed during a cursory inspection of the place.

Picking up on my sudden interest, Benson shot me a curious glance. "What is it?"

"Look at the cross. What do you notice?"

I gestured to the wooden crucifix mounted in the lavishly appointed dining area. I had not taken the high-powered lawyer as a religious man, so the presence of the Christian symbol had immediately jumped out at me. The cross hung above a distressed, farmhouse-style dining table large enough to seat six guests.

Benson let out a low whistle, his eyes widening ever so slightly. "The cross is upside down," he noted.

I nodded gravely. Some people believed the inverted cross to be demonic. Others referred to it as St. Peter's cross. The saint had been nailed to an upside-down cross, not believing himself worthy to be crucified in the same manner as Christ was. The scar on my chest—a souvenir of my encounter with the demon Morgal twenty years earlier—burned slightly as I leaned closer, confirming that the inverted cross held a whiff of demonic energy.

"What do you make of it?" Benson asked.

Good question. Had Davison's attacker inverted the cross as a signature of some sort, or was something else going here? My curiosity piqued, my gaze continued to roam the apartment. I retraced my steps, returning to all the other rooms I'd passed through earlier, willing myself to look at them with fresh eyes. Had I missed anything else?

My thoughts broke off as my searching gaze landed on the plush Persian carpet which decorated the hardwood living room floor. Intricate patterns adorned the rug, the abstract imagery of color and form pleasing to the eye. The mark of Morgal ached again, suggesting that something might be amiss. I kneeled, my gaze following the carpet's decorative lines...

And that's when the image hidden within the intricate weave revealed itself to me. A muscular human torso became recognizable, wings sprouting from powerful shoulders. A horned goat's head dominated the rippling physique. Someone had woven the lines of a demon into the carpet's pattern, visible when viewed from just the right angle.

Following a sudden hunch, I pulled the corner of the rug up, and my worst suspicions were confirmed. Occult glyphs and runes were etched in the wooden floor.

A stunned Benson sidled up to me and traced the strange symbols with his fingers. A bead of perspiration pearled on his forehead, inspiring me to wipe the sweat from my own brow. It suddenly felt like someone had turned up the heat in the penthouse apartment.

"You think the killer did this?"

I shook my head. I could accept the killer leaving one signature behind, but not three. Besides, the carpet had to have been custom-made by the victim, which only left one possibility to my mind.

"I think Davison was a devil worshipper."

5

Lawyers had a reputation of being soulless bloodsuckers, but I'd never come across one who actually prayed at the altar of evil. Then again, most occultists didn't advertise their ties to the dark side. Robert Davison had been targeted by a paranormal entity of some kind, most likely a demon. Considering his involvement with the dark arts, it added up. Dabbling with the occult often backfired on the user. Who knows what had driven Davison toward the darkness—greed was my best guess—but it had cost him dearly.

The big question was whether we were dealing with an isolated incident here—one demon turning on his would-be master—or if something bigger was brewing on the horizon. Time would tell. My churning gut and burning scar suggested this was far from over.

I promised Benson to stay in touch and made my way

back to the loft. I needed to run the case by Skulick and see what he would make of it. As always, I'd taken extensive pictures of the demonic paraphernalia at Davison's apartment. I hoped my partner might be able to put his encyclopedic knowledge of the occult to good use. Beyond identifying the demonic symbols, I couldn't make heads or tails out of the strange markings in the dead lawyer's apartment. Compared to Skulick, I was but a rank amateur when it came to this stuff.

As I stepped into our loft, I sensed something was wrong. Skulick didn't greet me, merely grunted and waved me over to his bank of computer monitors.

"What is it?" I asked, trepidation in my voice. I was starting to get a bad feeling about my partner's somber mood.

"There's been a development. We have an Archer sighting."

For a beat, the room tilted and blood rushed to my ears. Had Archer finally taken a life?

"What happened?" I said, my voice an emotionless whisper.

"You need to see this for yourself."

I nodded and eased up to Skulick's desk. His face was a grave mask, and it didn't bode well for what he was about to show me. I shoved the rooftop murder case to the back of my mind, my full attention fixed on my partner and the bad news he was about to dump on me.

To my surprise, he pulled up YouTube and clicked on a channel dedicated to myths and urban legends. Some of this stuff had been debunked decades ago. Bigfoot, Loch Ness, and UFO sightings dominated the channel.

Skulick selected a video titled "*Real Vampires.*"

"The video I'm about to play was posted late last night and has been spreading like wildfire online."

Skulick wasn't kidding. The video already had tens of thousands of views and hundreds of comments.

Before I could say anything else, Skulick tapped the play button. On-screen, the point of view of a moving, GoPro-style camera filled the screen. The camera swayed back and forth as the person carrying it rapidly advanced toward a looming structure. It appeared to be an abandoned factory building of some kind, pale sunlight dappling the worn exterior.

As the video drew closer to the dilapidated building, an arm appeared in the frame, gun in hand. The cameraman was hunting. All of a sudden, it felt like I was following the action in a first-person shooter.

The moving camera paused abruptly, turning toward a uniformed police officer who also sported a drawn firearm.

I was looking at police body cam footage taken by the first officer. As soon as I made the connection, the police officer with the body cam resumed his approach. The feed continued to sway wildly as he ran, the majestic skyline of the Cursed City bleakly outlined behind the industrial stretch of warehouses.

I watched, my gut churning with sick anticipation, as the officer and his partner entered the decaying factory building. Debris littered the ground, the walls bleeding graffiti. Gangs, taggers, and homeless had claimed the old factory as their own.

The cops tried to stay calm, but I could almost hear their hammering hearts, the tension and adrenaline evident through the shaky camera in their erratic movements and clipped verbal exchanges. The two officers expected trouble.

The nausea-inducing camera ride continued. The two men entered a cavernous chamber. Rusting steel rafters dangled from the ceiling, shadows bathed a catwalk of pipes, ventilation ducts, and old electrical cables. A tangle of rotting machinery dominated the floor. This had to be the factory's main floor.

The camera swept the space in a smooth pan, the officer's pace slower and more cautious now. A shadowy silhouette loomed before the cops.

As the man with the body cam drew closer, details became visible. The figure was wearing a pair of torn, ragged jeans and a black hoodie, a shadow come to spooky life. He was sitting Indian style at the center of the dust-caked factory floor. Only when the hooded figure peered up and the inhumanly pale features grew visible did I realize that I was staring at a vampire.

It wasn't Archer.

"Freeze! Do Not move!" the cop bellowed.

Naturally, the grinning bastard rose to his feet. Unkempt strands of hair poked from the hood, his alabaster skin forming a sharp contrast against the hoodie's black material.

A sick smile flitted over the vampire's face, and his eyes took on a dark tinge. These cops had no idea what they were up against, and a part of me wished I could avert my gaze, knowing all too well what was in store for the two officers. But I couldn't look away.

"I SAID FREEZE!"

The hooded figure's eyes narrowed into pinpoints of red, and I caught my first glimpse of the razor-sharp fangs. A beat later, the figure leapt toward the second cop, the one who wasn't wearing the body cam, and the world turned into a mad carousel ride from hell. Bestial sounds echoed, gunshots reverberated, panicked shouts rang through the factory.

The spooky figure tore into the hapless officer, knocking his pistol aside before burying his razor-sharp fangs into the man's throat.

Blood sprayed as the cop let out a series of gurgling sounds.

"Oh my God, oh my God, oh my God..."

The cop with the body camera seemed to be having a meltdown, the angle low to the floor as if he'd dropped to his knees, his voice little more than a terrified whisper.

The vampire fed for a beat before he tossed the first officer aside. The creature's full attention now riveted to the officer sporting the cam, exposed fangs dripping scarlet. There was no doubt as to what the creature would do next.

I braced myself for the attack as the officer with the cam lost his cool for good. He unleashed a wild fusillade of bullets as the vampire pounced, murder in its inhuman gaze.

Everybody knows that bullets can't harm a vampire.

But dumb luck favored the cop.

A few of the stray bullets punched through a grime-encrusted window and blazing sunlight shafted into the factory. The beams of pale sunlight engulfed the fast approaching vamp, and the ivory complexion beneath the black hoodie erupted in smoke. Albino flesh welted and turned black, the sound of sizzling skin drowned out by the monstrous roar of agony coming from the vampire.

The wailing creature turned away from the cop, survival instincts overcoming the creature's raging bloodlust. As the vamp darted out of the path of the searing sunlight, seeking cover behind the factory machinery, the officer continued his rapid retreat. Who knows what the cops had expected to find in the desolate factory, but it sure as hell hadn't been an undead bloodsucker.

Panicked breathing rasped hauntingly over the cam's audio as the officer cut a hasty retreat, prey desperately trying to outrun a superior predator.

He surged down the garbage-strewn corridor, the shaking cam creating the illusion that the footage had been recorded on a skipper at high tide.

I held my breath, utterly engrossed in the terrifying drama unfolding before my very eyes.

For a moment, it seemed like the cop would make it out of the factory alive, and I couldn't help but cross my fingers for the guy. He had almost reached the exit when a figure peeled from the deep shadows and blocked his escape.

I gasped, my blood turning to ice. Skulick shot me a concerned look.

The figure visible in the grainy body cam shot was intimately familiar to me. Archer was staring back at the cop, hair wild, skin white as marble, her eyes gleaming dangerously. She stepped into the dim light and the officer backed away from this second monster. Archer's lips sprouted fangs, and the officer's prayers turned into desperate pleas for his life.

"Please, nooo..."

Archer surged toward him with the ferocity of the

inhuman predator she'd become, and the cam became a blur of bloody imagery punctuated by the man's screams.

Mercifully, the screen went black.

My hands knotted into fists, nails digging into my sweaty palms. I had clung to the childish notion that Archer might've found a way to resist the dark curse, that all this time she hadn't allowed the black blood pumping through her veins to corrupt her. The video shattered all such foolish delusions. The Archer I'd fallen in love with was gone. A terrible beast had taken her place. It was up to me to hunt her down. And put an end to her for good.

6

I entered the abandoned factory featured in the YouTube vampire video, hand resting on *Hellseeker,* my senses alert. Broken glass crunched under my feet as I eased deeper into the ghostly maze of rotting machinery. The shadows around me seemed to move, my imagination getting the best of me.

Two hours had passed since I first watched the vampire video.

Two hours since my life had been turned upside-down again.

Locating the factory from the video had not proven to be too difficult. As soon as we'd finished watching the disturbing piece of reality TV, Skulick had proceeded to put his detective skills to good use.

Within an hour of surfing the web and making a few

phone calls with his contacts at the force, he'd produced the names of the two cops from the online horror show.

Officers John Palmbrook and Darryl Johnson were the two unfortunate souls who'd become the latest statistics in the ongoing battle with the forces of darkness. Their bodies were being examined at the coroner's office, and I was willing to bet the official cause of death would be "wild animal attack."

Both officers had decided to check out the old factory the other night after being tipped off by one their contacts. Word on the street was that the old factory had become a hotbed for drug activity. Well, someone had gotten that part wrong. The poor officers had walked into a nightmare beyond their realm of experience.

Before his death, Officer Johnson had managed to call for back-up. By the time the cavalry showed up on the scene, the vampires were long gone.

As the bodies of the two officers arrived in the morgue, the forensic team quickly realized that the body cam was missing. Nobody gave it too much thought until a few hours later when the video ended up trending online. While the force's cyber forensics team was hard at work identifying the original IP address from which the video had been uploaded, mirror sites continued to pop up online at an alarming rate.

There was no doubt in my mind that the vampires must've uploaded the body cam video, but that raised an interesting question. Why would they want to draw attention to themselves like that? Vampires had spent centuries convincing the world that they were myths, so why reveal themselves now and risk a direct confrontation with humanity? The more I racked my brain over it, the more I became convinced that I was missing an important piece of the puzzle.

My burning need for answers ultimately led me to the scene of the crime. I wasn't sure what I hoped to find here. Archer and the other vampire would be long gone, but I had to start somewhere.

It didn't take me long to locate the blood spatter on the floor where the first vampire had launched into the hapless officer. I bit back my rising anger at the grisly sight and focused on the other details of the scene. The rotting machinery and graffiti-streaked walls were a far cry from the traditional gothic setting most people might associate with creatures of the night. Why had the vampires sought refuge in this godforsaken industrial wasteland? The most obvious explanation was that they were trying to keep a low profile and stay off the radar. But that brought me back to my original question: Why post a video of their exploits for the whole world to see?

I must've spent a good two hours combing the factory floor, desperate to find anything that might lead me to Archer. My efforts turned out to be in vain. I inhaled a lot of dust, spotted a fair share of rats and came across a nice collection of empty beer bottles and fast food wrappers. The city's homeless population had turned the factory into their own version of motel 6 until the vamps moved in.

Doing my best to fight off my growing feeling of defeat, I left the old factory and headed back to my car. My next stop was the coroner's office, where I planned to examine the bodies of the two dead officers.

As the factory receded in my rear-view mirror, my eyes kept traveling to the rows upon rows of abandoned tenements alongside the battered road. When the city had lost much of its manufacturing industry ten years earlier, this area had spiraled into economic decline. Nowadays the lost souls of the city called this place their home now—gangs, homeless, prostitutes—and now vampires had moved into the neighborhood.

The inhuman blood keeping Archer alive had steered her toward others of her kind. There was no such thing as a "good" vampire, but some were more brutal and vicious than others. Who knew what kind of diabolical crowd she'd fallen in with? Suddenly every building in the desolate neighborhood represented a potential hiding place for a nest of bloodsuckers.

It took me about a half an hour to reach the coroner's office. I'd briefly touched base with Benson earlier and told him I wanted to look at the bodies of the dead officers. To my surprise, he didn't refuse my request. In fact, he'd offered me anything to bring Archer in. Witnessing one of his best detectives feeding on another officer had gutted him. Like me, he wanted us to wrap up this case as speedily as possible.

My footsteps echoed creepily as I entered the morgue. Frank Casey, the corner, barely acknowledged me, too preoccupied with the latest murder victim on his stainless-steel table. Casey's full head of hair was turning gray, but he was tan and looked like he stuck to a regular exercise regimen. I guess facing death every day provided plenty of motivation to embrace a healthy lifestyle.

Like so many other people in law enforcement that I ran into, he didn't quite know what to make of the rumpled demon hunter who'd been assisting the force ever since the Crimson Circle incident. I bit my tongue and played along, allowing him to finish what he was doing in silence.

Once done, he led me to the bodies. As expected, the dead officers didn't make for a pretty sight, their bodies lacerated with grisly bite marks. Forget the twin puncture wounds found in the latest Hollywood vampire flicks—these men had been ravaged and mauled before their blood was drained. They looked more like shark attack victims than extras from *The Vampire Diaries*.

I inched closer to the two corpses and sighed inwardly when my demonic scar didn't flare up with pain. The reason behind my visit was twofold. I was interested in hearing what forensics might've found during their examination of the bodies, but I was also worried that the two dead officers might be infected by the vampiric curse. If they'd been turned, they would rise as undead beasts as soon as the sun went down. Morgal's mark wasn't setting off any alarm bells, so I figured we were in the clear on that one.

As the coroner went into specifics, my mind tuned out his clinical description of their many wounds. My medical knowledge is limited to reruns of *ER*. The sight of the two savaged officers dominated my thoughts to a point where all else faded into the background. What was the matter with me? I'd seen hundreds of victims over the years, many far worse than the mauled cops. So why was this affecting me in such a profound manner?

The answer was simple. Archer had killed one of them, which meant my own foolish actions had set this horror show in motion.

"You might find it interesting that I discovered petroleum hydrocarbons and a series of heavy metals on the uniforms of both officers."

The coroner's latest words broke my trance and I peered up at him.

"Do I finally have your attention now?" The coroner appraised me coolly. Judging by the superior tone in his voice, he probably thought I was high on something. Or maybe just stupid.

"Hydrocarbons and heavy metals?" I said.

The coroner nodded. "Petroleum hydrocarbons, to be exact. They're contained in gasoline, diesel fuels, and motor oil. I also found trace amounts of lead, cadmium, mercury, zinc, nickel, and copper. My guess is the attackers had contact with these contaminants."

I frowned at the man, still trying to wrap my head around his words. "Are you telling me the killers worked at a garage?"

"Close. Perhaps a facility or factory which handles motor vehicles but has fallen into serious disrepair. Most places still in operation wouldn't allow for such high levels of contaminants..."

The coroner's voice grew distant once again, my mind wheeling. On my way to the factory, I'd passed an abandoned car wrecking yard. The place had given me the creeps. I suddenly had a strong hunch where Archer and her new vampire friends might be hiding.

7

"You may kiss the bride," the priest declared.

About time, Skulick thought as his beautiful Michelle raised her white veil and leaned forward. She was resplendent, an angelic vision in her white wedding dress.

How did a bum like him deserve to get so lucky? Michelle was one in a million. Beautiful yet down-to-earth, whip smart with a playful sense of humor. And she understood that being a homicide detective was more than a job, it was a calling.

It had taken him only a few dates to know that she was the one, and now he'd get to spend the rest of his life with the stunning brunette.

Babe, I love you with all my heart, he thought as their lips locked in a passionate kiss. After what seemed like an eternity, he pulled away from his beloved and... froze.

Dread welled up in him, and he recoiled with instinctive revulsion.

Michelle's wedding gown was streaked with blood. More blood was smeared across her face. Worse than that was the terrible hunger in Michelle's inhuman gaze. The twin fangs poking from her lips dripped scarlet.

Skulick touched his neck and gasped with shock when his fingers came away red. The blood coating Michelle's bridal gown was his own.

As this terrible realization sank in, he turned to the priest for help. But the father of the cloth had transformed into something else, a creature of the night with alabaster features framed by long black hair and eyes blazing with an unholy fire.

Michelle tore into him, apparently determined to drain him fully. As the transformed priest's terrible laughter reverberated in the suddenly deserted church, Skulick screamed…

SKULICK'S EYES FLICKERED OPEN, and the waking world cast aside the nightmare in an explosion of flashing computer monitors. His reflection played across one of the screens, his face coated in sweat, looking worn and haggard.

He took a deep breath, reality snapping back into focus. He must've dozed off at his desk. He had been pushing himself past his limits to find a cure for Archer. Unfortunately, his body couldn't quite keep up with his tireless mind. These involuntary naps had become more common with each passing day.

And so had the nightmares. They were always the same. A wedding that had never happened, a love he failed to save. Painful glimpses of a life never lived. And lurking in the background, the terrifying presence of the vampire who had taken his Michelle from him.

Marek.

The past thirty years had failed to erase the memory of the diabolical master vampire, but at least the dreams had become less frequent. That all changed a month ago when Archer succumbed to the same affliction as Michelle. Seeing Raven lose the woman he loved broke Skulick's heart and reopened all the old wounds. There had to be a way to save Archer. To spare Raven the pain of having to destroy his love.

Skulick worried about Raven. Had he made the right choice when he pulled Richard's son into this crazy war against the darkness? There was no other way, he told himself. Raven's grief and pain over the loss of his parents needed to be channeled into something positive. Better to train the young boy and prepare him for the battles ahead. Hell would not rest until the son of the greatest monster hunter who ever lived was dead.

Of course, Raven had made plenty of infernal enemies

of his own over the years. The boy was a chip off the old block.

He'd given Raven a fighting chance against Hell's legions, but could he save Raven from his own demons? Raven had lost so much; adding Archer to the list might break him. Not right away, but in time the guilt would consume him. The drinking and bar skirmishes were just the beginning. He couldn't let Raven go down this dark path. Skulick knew all too well what lay at the end of it.

With a heavy heart, Skulick wheeled himself to the coffee maker and poured himself a steaming cup of joe. The black brew burned down his throat and made him feel like a human being again. Outside, rain pelted the skylight, erasing the world from view. Distant, incessant traffic drifted from the streets below, sounding like the city's weakening heartbeat.

If the forces of darkness got their way, the Cursed City's sick heart would stop beating forever one of these days.

Not on my watch, Skulick thought.

Eight months earlier, during a routine investigation of a haunted hotel, a vengeful spirit had caught him off guard and dropped him out a window. The three-story fall had robbed him of the use of his legs but not his calling to protect the world from demons. Losing his ability to walk had been traumatic, but like the loss of his fiancée three decades earlier, he'd found a way to bury the pain deep inside. He locked it away and focused on making the best of his situation. Research had become his weapon, the vast occult library his war machine. He steepled his hands, peered through the rain-washed window, and waited. He was expecting a visitor. A very special visitor.

He didn't have to wait long.

A beeping sound signaled the arrival of his guest. He swiveled toward one of the CCTV screens that offered a view of the loft's main entrance. A tall, athletic looking man stood in the rain, the collar of the black coat turned up and a heavy leather satchel in one hand. He carried an umbrella, but it did a piss poor job of keeping him dry.

Skulick flicked a switch and the camera zoomed in on the person waiting below. The sun had carved deep grooves into the man's tanned skin, but there was a strength there. A mane of gray hair spilled down the priestly collar. Father Ignatius looked more like an aging rock star than a man of the cloth. His eyes flickered with impatience as they looked back at him through the security camera.

"Are you going to let me in or do you want me to catch my death out here?"

Skulick hesitated for a beat. Experience had taught him it was unwise to welcome guests into his inner sanctum. Father Ignatius was member of the White Crescent, a special branch of Vatican-trained exorcists dedicated to fighting demons and monsters. Even though they'd fought side by side on multiple occasions over the years, old habits were hard to shake. But there were times when exceptions had to be made.

Skulick tapped his keyboard, and the main entrance buzzed open. Ignatius was a demon hunter, a profession that carried certain risks. One of them was possession. Skulick recalled a tale where a demon hitched a ride in an exorcist and tried to breach the Vatican and murder the Pope. The loft's protective wards would detect any such inhuman passenger—or so he hoped.

Since the loss of his legs, the loft had become both his fortress and his prison. Venturing beyond the walls of the converted warehouse was fraught with risk. His handicap would make him a tempting target for his old demonic enemies. But locking himself away from the world had raised his sense of paranoia. If it wasn't for Raven, he truly would be a crazy hermit trapped in a castle filled with the dark ghosts of his past.

Skulick nervously drummed his fingers against his desk as Ignatius stepped into the elevator. None of the wards came to life, and Skulick exhaled a deep sigh of relief. He hadn't told Raven about this meeting. He didn't want to get the kid's hopes up. Ignatius had traveled all the way from Rome, bearing a special gift.

The exorcist wasn't merely carrying his demon hunting kit in his black leather case, but also a potential cure for vampirism.

The elevator doors rumbled open and the priest strode into the loft, leaving a trail of water in his wake.

"It's been a long time, old friend," Ignatius said.

"Too long." Skulick said, finally lowering his guard. This was his first meeting with Ignatius since the accident, and he saw the priest's eyes soften with sympathy as they swept over the wheelchair.

"Looks like the chair hasn't slowed you down a bit."

"My young protégée has been nice enough to pick up some of the slack."

"So I hear. He's getting quite the reputation."

Skulick flashed his old friend a warm smile. "How are things in Rome?"

"Great food, even greater people. And don't get me started on the weather. This rain is killing me. How do you stand it?"

"I'm a homebody nowadays." There was a slightly embarrassed pause before Skulick said, "I heard about the incident in Liguria. Something about demons taking over a convent?"

Ignatius' eyebrows ticked upward and he rubbed his chin. "And how would you know about that? The Vatican has gone to great lengths to keep a lid on the *incident*."

"I have my sources." Skulick pointed at his bank of flickering terminals.

Skulick offered Ignatius a cup of his infamously strong

coffee. The exorcists took a deep swig from the steaming brew and a smile lit up his face.

"You haven't lost your magic touch. It's almost perfect."

Skulick arched an eyebrow. "Almost?"

Ignatius pulled out a flask from his coat and added a shot to his coffee. He took another sip, and pleasure lit up his face. Skulick found himself smiling, too.

"It's great to see you, Ignatius. You're looking good, old friend."

Ignatius smiled. "That's a lie, but I appreciate it anyway. We're getting older—and, unlike my Scotch, not necessarily better."

"Hey, speak for yourself."

"I will keep fighting the darkness to the bitter end," Ignatius said, determination in his voice. "Until the day I fall and the next fool takes my place. Fortunately, you seem to have found your successor. Richard's boy has been making quite a name for himself."

"He still has a thing or two to learn."

"Don't we all." Ignatius nodded thoughtfully.

"Did you bring me what I asked for?" Skulick inquired.

"I'm here, aren't I?"

The exorcist lifted his black leather satchel and placed in on a nearby chair. A brilliant white light emanated from inside the bag as he opened it. With great care, Ignatius extricated a small bottle shaped like a cross. The bottle—or rather the liquid inside—was the source of the light. "I hope you appreciate all the favors I had to call in to get you this."

"I do, old friend. But I also plan on holding up my end of the bargain."

Skulick reached out for the shimmering bottle. The white light bathed his face with a pleasant, soothing warmth.

"Not many men have ever laid their eyes on angel blood before. The only known cure for vampirism."

Skulick took the cross-bottle into his hand. He sensed the exorcist's hesitation to give it up, but Ignatius finally relented. They both gazed at it for a long moment. The light seemed to call out to them both, demanding their attention.

"Don't look at it too long. Men have gone blind doing so," Ignatius warned.

Skulick had heard many a rumor about the angelic blood that was safely kept under lock and key at the headquarters of the White Crescent in Rome. According to the legends he'd discovered in medieval texts, an angel had fought side by side with the members of the White Crescent and had fallen in a terrible battle with an invading demon horde. Before the angel perished, the order had managed to preserve some of the divine being's life force.

Over the next few centuries, the White Crescent had come to discover many of the blood's miraculous properties.

One of them was its ability to cure an afflicted from the vampiric curse. How he wished he would have known about the angel blood decades earlier when Richard had been forced to stake his beloved when she tried to murder him.

Skulick had no idea how much of the divine essence remained in Rome, but the vial only contained enough of the holy life force to save one afflicted soul.

Despite their long friendship, Ignatius had to answer to his order which meant they couldn't offer up such a precious relic for free. There were many miracles inside the vault one floor above them, and it held at least one item that the White Crescent desperately wanted. A book that had been in Skulick's possession for over a decade. A book with the power to alter the fate of humanity if it should fall into the wrong hands.

With a sense of wariness, he handed Ignatius the heavy, leather-bound tome that had been sitting on his desk throughout their conversation. The *Daemonium* contained the names of all the demons in Hell. According to legend, there were only two copies left in the whole world. As the story went, if both copies should be reunited, the gates of Hell would open. Was there any truth to these myths? Skulick generally tried to err on the side of caution. That's why he had secured the volume—and why he felt so guilty about giving it up.

You don't have a choice buddy, he told himself. He

wanted, *needed* to save Detective Jane Archer so he could save Raven.

Mind made up, he shook hands with the priest, sealing their deal. Father Ignatius placed the infernal book in his leather satchel and zipped it up. The bag was protected by powerful white magic. Even if the satchel should somehow fall into the wrong hands, only a member of the White Crescent would be able to open it. Skulick trusted them to keep the book safe, but he still trusted himself more.

Business out of the way, Ignatius spent another hour reminiscing about their past adventures before he left to catch his flight. Hell's agents didn't rest and their work never stopped. Another mission awaited Ignatius on the West Coast, where the daughter of a movie producer was being tormented by demonic forces.

With Ignatius gone, Skulick was gripped with renewed regret. Had he done the right thing by giving up the *Daemonium*? As the light from the angel blood washed over him, he prayed he hadn't made a terrible mistake.

8

The abandoned auto wrecking yard loomed before me, a foreboding eyesore in a neighborhood full of them. A ten-foot-tall chain link fence topped with barbed wire enclosed the cemetery of rusting steel and gutted machinery. Faded signs warned trespassers of potential prosecution.

I doubted it would stop anyone intent on entering the junk yard, especially considering the non-existent police presence in this forsaken part of the city. Like the nearby factory, the place had been abandoned during the latest recession, and most locals avoided the spooky scrapyard at all costs. Folks had a funny way of disappearing around the place.

The junkyard is haunted, man, one of the bums I'd questioned had said as I offered him a smoke. The homeless man wasn't that far off the mark if vampires had indeed turned the wasteland of junked cars into their personal hunting ground.

Sunlight beat down on me as I approached the fence with a sense of growing trepidation. It was around one o'clock, which gave me about another five hours before nightfall. Even though *Hellseeker* was as effective against vamps as stakes, I had no idea how many of the monsters I might be up against. Venturing into a potential nest of bloodsuckers was never a smart move, but at least I had daylight on my side. At night, this would have been suicide mission.

My phone buzzed in my pocket, but I ignored it. Skulick had been trying to reach me for the last hour, but I refused to answer my cell. I knew he would do his best to talk me out my latest craziness. Vampires made him more than nervous, understandably enough, and he would always err on the side of caution when it came to these monsters. But I was a man possessed, desperate for closure. I needed to confront my own demons before my resolve wavered.

By turning Archer into a vampire, I had doomed her to an unholy purgatory between life and death. It was up to me to set her free.

I reached the fence and took a deep breath. The stench of gasoline clotted the thick air and raked my lungs.

I extricated a wire cutter from my trench coat and went to work on the chain link gate. Metal quickly gave way, and I carved a hole into the fence big enough for me to fit through.

I slipped through the jagged opening and entered a wasteland of broken glass, mangled engine parts, and cars piled up helter-skelter. Hydraulic compactors sat abandoned like exotic technology left behind by a race of ancient alien invaders.

As I moved deeper in to the wrecking yard, my scar began to heat up. No doubt about it, black magic had found a home among the ruins of these savaged vehicles.

Following my instincts, I approached a row of parked cars that formed a bulwark of rusting steel. Studying the wall of faded metal, I couldn't shake the feeling that the trunks had become makeshift steel coffins for these urban vamps.

My scar itching something fierce now, I stepped up to the first vehicle, a '99 Ford Mustang that had seen better days, its red paint job having taken a serious beating from the elements.

I circled the Mustang and peered inside the shadow-cloaked vehicle. The scent of moldy leather assaulted my nostrils as I pried open the creaking car door and I found the latch that would open the trunk. *Hellseeker* ready in one hand, I steeled myself for what lay ahead.

Here goes nothing, I thought.

I popped the trunk, and within seconds a bestial roar reverberated across the wrecking yard. Guess my instincts had been right, but there was no time to celebrate.

A human shape burst from the open trunk, smoke erupting from the hoodie-sporting figure. He whirled toward me, eyes wild, fangs visible in the glare of sunlight.

Having identified the cause of its terrible agony, the vampire attacked. I squeezed the trigger and drilled two blessed bullets into the monster.

The projectiles stopped the vampire dead cold in its tracks. It stumbled backward under the onslaught before dissolving into a swirling cloud of flaming ash.

For a beat I just stood there, rooted in place, face masked in perspiration, my heart hammering a mile a minute, almost expecting more of the car trunks to pop open and reveal an army of the first vampire's undead brethren. But no such thing happened.

I was surrounded by monsters, but they were at rest now, unaware of the foolish mortal who planned to interrupt their vampiric slumber.

Still considering my next move, an animalistic growl cut through the junkyard. The sound made the hairs on my back stand up.

Adrenaline pumping, I turned around.

Two hundred pounds of salivating Rottweiler glared back at me. The four-legged guardian flashed its jagged teeth and was rapidly joined by three other dogs who looked like they were all too eager to tear me apart.

I should have guessed the vampires would have guardians of some kind. I hated shooting an animal, even one who was planning on taking big, bloody chunks out of me. The dogs were doing what they had been taught to do—protect their masters.

Four against one—the odds were not in my favor. That said, I wouldn't let them rip me in pieces without a fight. Even if I managed to kill one or two of the dogs, their sheer numbers would overwhelm me. Once the blood started to flow, these beasts would be as unstoppable as the horde of vampires they protected. Retreat was in order.

I scanned my surroundings as I inched away from the growling canines. There was no obvious path to escape. Any moment now, the animals would explode into ferocious motion. I had to get away from them. Now!

Giving myself an internal push, I spun around while firing a few rounds at the ground, hoping it would scare the dogs away.

They backed off slightly as clouds of dust erupted at their feet but their growls didn't abate, their eyes staying fixed on me. They must've been exposed to gunfire during their training. *Great!*

An instant later, the dogs loped toward me, and I ran for my life.

Riding a wave of adrenaline, I leapt onto the trunk of

one of the cars, desperate to attain the high ground. Jaws snapped at me and caught the fabric of my pants.

I lost my balance and stumbled backward, finding myself face to face with one of the slavering beasts. My fist shot out and connected with the dog's snout. The salivating beast let out a pitiful whelp.

Sorry, guy, but you left me no choice.

Before another one of the Rottweilers could tear into me, I climbed onto the car's roof. Weathered metal creaked and groaned under my feet.

The massive Rottweilers circled the vehicle, jaws snapping at the air in bloodthirsty anticipation.

As one of them scrambled onto the vehicle, I launched myself at the roof of the neighboring car. The dogs tried to follow, but they kept slipping on the metal, unable to maintain their balance.

I had escaped for the moment, but they were smart and determined. The dogs would find a way up, or else they'd simply keep me trapped up here until their masters awoke.

Scanning the car cemetery, my eyes landed on a nearby building that must have been the wrecking yard's main office back in the day. The row of gutted vehicles extended all the way up to the structure in question. If I kept jumping from car to car, I could work my way up to one of the building's dirt-caked windows.

Plan in place, I advanced toward the building by

leaping from one rusty car to the next. The phalanx of Rottweilers tracked my progress, patiently waiting for me to lose my balance and turn into their new favorite chewy toy.

After hop-skipping across a dozen cars, I somehow reached the office building.

I wrapped my coat around my hand and punched a hole through the window. Shards rained down on me as I reached through the hole and located the latch on the other side. A beat later, I opened the window and slipped into the building. I could almost feel the Rottweilers disappointment as they watched me disappear.

The good news was that I had managed to get away from the dogs. But I was still trapped. The sole way out of the wrecking yard was past those ravenous dogs. And their numbers seemed to be growing with each passing minute. I counted about seven of the beasts now.

Vampires had used both human and animal guardians since the beginning of time. Formidable creatures at night, they had learned to rely on other predators to keep them safe while they were at their most vulnerable.

I peered out at the car cemetery, knowing all too well that Archer—or at least the thing Archer had turned into—was out there somewhere. Lost in the sleep of the damned, waiting to rise as soon as the sun vanished behind the horizon.

I checked the time. Getting close to two o'clock. I still had about four hours before sunset. Plenty of time to find a way of this place, right?

My best bet was to ring Skulick and have him send Benson and the troops into the junkyard. That's what I should have done in the first place, but I'd allowed my emotions to get the best of me—something that was quickly becoming an unfortunate pattern.

I whipped out my cell. No signal. Perfect.

I turned the phone off and on, but the results remained the same. Had these vampires resorted to a few other black magic tricks to secure their nest? Or had they gone high tech and set up a cell phone jammer?

Speculating about it was a waste of time. I was trapped and couldn't expect any outside help. Refusing to get caught up in a bout of self-recrimination about going at it alone—that would come later once Skulick discovered what I'd been up to and chewed me out—I tried to steer my mind into a more constructive direction.

My gaze roamed the wrecking yard while the massive Rottweilers gnashed their teeth and launched a salvo of barks at me. They seemed to be mocking me, waiting eagerly for me to be stupid enough to venture beyond the safety of the main building.

Even though part of me felt tempted to make a run for it, I knew better. I couldn't outpace the pack. After besting demons and ghosts for all of my adult life, getting torn to shreds by a bunch of junkyard dogs would be a sad way to go.

"Raven!"

The voice made me whirl, a shiver crawling up my spine. It sounded exactly like Archer. My panicky gaze searched the pools of shadows, expecting my would-be girlfriend to peel from the darkness with fangs bared.

No such thing happened.

Hellseeker leveled, I took a cautious step into the encroaching blackness.

I weaved past desks and office chairs in the main office space, making sure to avoid the obstacle course of junk carpeting the floor. Dust danced in the air, illuminated by a sickly gray light seeping through the dirty windows. Could some of the vampires be hiding out within the walls of this building? Anything was possible, but the burning sensation in my chest had subsided.

I reached the end of the main office and froze as I picked up a muffled coughing sound. I sure as hell wasn't alone in the building. The sound had emanated from behind the closed door up ahead.

I steadied my breathing, cleared my mind, and kicked the door open. The room was empty except for the naked, bald man sitting cross-legged at its center.

The man stared at me with haunted eyes, his ascetic

features pale and skeletal in the light knifing through a grime-encrusted skylight. Gaunt and raw-boned, the man's once-powerful build had been stripped bare of every ounce of fat, almost as if some sick freak had been trying to starve him to death. Morgal's mark failed to respond to the man's presence, suggesting that whoever this spooky looking fella might be, he wasn't a vampire.

I cautiously approached, finger whitening on the trigger. The mysterious man might not be a creature of the night, but there was something weird about him.

As I drew closer, I took note of a faded pattern of strange occult tattoos decorating the man's body. And then I noticed the scars. Vampire bite marks lined every square inch of his exposed anatomy. His neck showed the worst damage. The undead bastards had been feeding on this poor soul for who knows how long.

"Help me," the pitiful figure pleaded, his voice a glassy whisper, slate-gray eyes fixed on me. There was a near hypnotic quality to his gaze. My temples pulsed, rage quickening my breath. The vampires had fed on the stranger for weeks, maybe months, draining him of his own life-force and will to live. Judging by his sorry state, it was a miracle he was still alive.

The man remained a statue as I closed in. I saw no restrains or chains, nothing that would explain why this rundown character figure hadn't tried to escape. Did the dogs keep him trapped in this building? Perhaps, but why had he barely moved since I entered the room?

I took another step and that's when both *Hellseeker* and the *Seal of Solomon*, my magical ring which could ward of the forces of darkness, lit up with a spectral green light.

That couldn't possibly be a good sign.

My gaze turned to the dusty floor, where the outline of a large circle and pentagram appeared. Both circle and pentagram flashed with a fiery, menacing pulse of energy.

A dark realization washed over me. I had stepped into a binding circle. Traps like this only worked on supernatural creatures. I understood now why the figure in front of me had not tried to escape. The bald man staring back at me wasn't human.

I was looking at a demon.

As soon as the thought slashed through my mind, the figure before me rose, somehow drawing energy from my presence.

With horror, I realized that by setting foot into the binding circle, my blessed weapons must've have broken the wards that kept the entity trapped within this chamber. the demon flashed me a cool smile, the first hint of life creeping into his gaunt features.

"Thank you, Raven."

A new strength and energy filled the demon's voice. His eyes lit up with an incandescent fire, and I instinctively squeezed the trigger. I hadn't survived this long as a monster hunter by engaging demons in prolonged chit-chat. Even a second of hesitation could spell the difference between life and death.

The roar of *Hellseeker* was deafening in the small space. But even though I'd moved as quickly as humanly possible, my reaction had come too late. The man—correction, demon—had vanished into thin air, and my blessed bullets bounced harmlessly against the wall. I swallowed hard, my face dripping sweat. What terrible evil had I inadvertently set free now?

My breath coming in sharp bursts, I spun around. There was no trace of the demon. I was alone again. Archer wasn't here—she'd never been here.

As my heart rate returned to normal, understanding dawned. The trapped demon had used his last reserves of power to probe my mind and lure me into the chamber with the sound of her voice. The demon must've known that my blessed weapons would break the magic seal that had kept him trapped in here for God knows how long. The holy power radiated by *Hellseeker* and the *Seal of Solomon* wasn't exactly subtle if you were tuned into the supernatural frequency. The demon had probably seen me coming from a block away.

I tore back into the main chamber of the building and froze. Fear surged at the grisly sight that awaited me. The main door was wide open, and the steaming carcasses of the dead Rottweilers were piled up on the filthy carpet, the scent of their blood filling the air.

Even in his emaciated state, the demon had cut a blood swath through the dogs. He must have torn the Rottweilers open and tossed them aside in a matter of seconds. But that was only part of the reason why my heart was pounding with naked terror. The light pouring through the open door had changed. A cloying darkness had settled over the wrecking yard.

Gripped by a terrible premonition, I sprinted toward the nearest window. As I peered outside, my heart sank. A pale moon was rising, painting the world outside in ominous shadows.

Somehow I'd lost hours when I breached the magical circle imprisoning the demon. It had felt like minutes to me, while in the real world at least four hours had passed. Black magic can warp space and time. That was one of the first lessons Skulick had drilled into me.

He'd also taught me never to run off alone or let my emotions draw me into a fight I couldn't win. Guess I should have paid better attention to my mentor when I'd had the chance.

A series of metallic creaks echoed through the night. I peered through the nearest window. Outside, the trunks of the rusting cars popped open one by one. Shadows bled from the vehicles, gaining shape and form as they poured into the moonlight.

Bile barbed the back of my throat, and I clenched my teeth as the vampires emerged from their makeshift coffins. They all wore ragged hoodies and torn cargo pants or jeans—street kids transformed into monstrous gods. Like a hungry school of sharks, they circled the office building, knowing all too well that a living, breathing human with blood pumping through his veins was hiding inside.

9

Death was closing in.

My eyes narrowed with the anticipation of violence. The weight of the blessed pistol in my hand provided meagre comfort, but I was glad to have it nonetheless.

The origin of my blessed weapon was another mystery in a world of unanswered questions. I wasn't even sure how it worked. All I knew was that the weapon had been forged from a magical sword and had served as my father's most important weapon in the battle with the dark side.

To the untrained eye, the gun looked to be a Beretta. And like that gun, it held fifteen 9mm rounds. The bullets themselves were standard issue; the ammo magically changed once fired, becoming a serious threat to the legions of darkness. *Hellseeker* didn't discriminate between demons, ghosts or vampires—it destroyed them all.

I'd used up a few bullets in the wrecking yard earlier when I tried to scare off the Rottweilers. Between my spare magazine and the bullets already loaded, I figured I had close to twenty-five rounds left. The mob of bloodsuckers zeroing in on the building had to number twice that. And that was an optimistic estimate.

I'm not a bad shot by any means, but even if I managed to take down one vamp with each of my remaining bullets, I'd still be outnumbered two dozen to one.

Not exactly the best odds.

I mentally ran through my options. Should I make a run for it and confront the undead horde in the maze of machinery outside? Or would I improve my chances by trying to hold off the advancing vampire tribe from inside the office building?

I decided on the second option. Outside in the darkness, the vampires' heightened senses and sheer numbers would easily overwhelm me. The night was their playground. Better to stay put. Within these walls, I would do my darnedest to pick off as many of the bloodsuckers as possible. At least until I ran out of ammo. I hoped they might back off once they realized the high price they'd have to pay to get their fangs in me.

Look at the bright side, kiddo, I told myself. *It's a full moon, so at least you can see the bloodsucking bastards.* I couldn't remember how many times in the past I'd wished my magical pistol came with a night-vision scope of some kind.

And you won't miss any of the gory details when they break in here and rip you apart.

Shit, I have bleak sense of humor.

I leaned out of the window and sighted down on the incoming vamps. My breath steadied and all sounds faded. My world was reduced to the green glowing gun in my hand and the advancing ring of monsters.

I waited for them to draw closer and step into my gun's effective range. I might not have enough ammo to shoot my way out of the wrecking yard, but I would make every bullet count.

Sweat trickled down my hair despite the cool wind. *Steady now...*

The first vampire had almost reached my position when I squeezed the trigger. The sound shattered the unearthly silence in the junkyard. A perfect black hole formed in the vamp's forehead. Black lines spiderwebbed across his face as the power of *Hellseeker* reacted with corrupted flesh. A beat later, the creature evaporated in a cloud of ash and fire.

One down, way too many to go.

Seeing the first of their ranks fall didn't slow down the monsters. In fact, it seemed to speed up their attack—and they were already moving fast.

I tried not to dwell on the fact that Archer was among

their numbers and squeezed off the next shot. A second vampire went supernova and turned into a whirlwind of ash. More vampires followed. Even as I took one down, another took its place. I was racking up a considerable body count, but my fusillade was barely slowing the vampires down.

As they drew nearer, the vampires slipped between the mass of car wrecks, dipping in and out of view. I tried to track them, my eyes darting everywhere at once. Amid the deafening roar of *Hellseeker*, I heard a different sound—a metallic creak that seemed to be coming from overhead.

They're on the roof, I thought, panic rising inside me. The sound of a window shattering made me whirl. There had been no time to secure the exits, no time to fortify my position. The vampires were breaching the building and all too soon would be upon me.

I moved toward the center of the main chamber, stepping behind one of the desks sagging under piles of junk. It provided lousy cover, but I'd take what I could get.

A shadow ahead of me moved. I reacted on instinct, my next bullet finding the intruder before he could attack.

A silhouette erupted from the darkness, backlit by a flash of fire, accompanied by an inhuman shriek.

The shadows bled ash.

I'd lost count of how many of the vampires I'd killed so far. Didn't matter. There were still too many of them and only one of me. I was making my last stand. All I could hope for was to take as many of the undead bastards with me a possible.

More shapes moved in the dark, and more succumbed to my bullets. The sudden click of the hammer falling on an empty chamber served as a sharp reminder that my ammo was limited.

I released the empty magazine and snapped in a fresh one. Not a moment too soon, as another vampire leapt at me.

But this time I didn't fire.

I couldn't.

Archer stepped into a pool of moonlight. Her transformation hadn't tainted her beauty. She moved like liquid, her skin flawless porcelain. An irrational, animal part of me wanted to cast my holy weapon aside and take her into my arms. Dark hair spilled down her ivory neck, framing the face I'd fallen for when I'd first laid eyes on it less than a year ago.

"Jane," I breathed. If she recognized her name, it didn't show on her face.

As Archer drew closer, I noticed a subtle but important difference in her appearance. The spark in her eyes was gone, the playful twinkle replaced by an unyielding, bottomless hunger.

I had dreaded this confrontation, had played it out in my mind's eye too many times to count. How would I react when I came face to face with the monster my foolish actions had created? Would I be strong enough to forget everything we had shared? Would I be able to pull the trigger and release Archer from this earthly Hell I'd condemned her to?

Well, the moment had finally arrived. And not surprisingly, I felt my resolve wavering. I found it impossible to pull the trigger.

"Archer, stay back..."

"Nice to see you again, lover."

The voice sent a shiver down my spine, and I forgot to breathe for a beat.

"Have you come to save me from the big bad vampires?"

The question hung in the air.

"I never..." my voice trailed off, the apology dying on my lips. "Or perhaps you came to put me out my misery? To save me from myself?" Her lips curled upward in a diabolical smile.

That was exactly what I'd come here to do, but I still didn't pull the trigger. I couldn't look away from her eyes. Vampires could hypnotize their victims, lulling their prey into helpless surrender. Part of me knew what she was doing. Part of me didn't care.

"I've been hoping you'd come for me. But not to set me free."

"Archer," I tried again, mumbling through numbed lips.

"Join us. Embrace the darkness and live forever."

Never, my mind screamed. But my body was saying something very different.

I lowered *Hellseeker*. Archer's mesmerizing sexuality had overwhelmed my mental defenses. I wanted those luscious lips to find my neck, for her to sink her fangs into me…

She took a step forward, her arms open wide.

Movement caught my eye, wrenching my gaze from hers for an instant.

It was enough to break the hypnotic spell she'd cast over me. I scowled and fired at the two vampires who'd materialized at Archer's side, dropping them both.

She hissed and darted away.

I continued firing into the darkness, the rest of my ammo impotently vanishing into the encroaching shadows.

Gun empty, I knew it was over. I'd reached the end of the road.

The ring of vampires realized it a second after I did. They closed in, grinning.

Archer led the way.

She took a confident step toward me.

It was poetic justice that she'd be the one to take my life.

Bracing myself for the inevitable, my lips set in a tight line.

I'm so sorry for this.

Hellseeker might be out of ammo, but I still had my protective talisman. My fist shot out, connected with Archer's alabaster cheek. She cried out in surprise as my blessed ring raised an angry welt on her skin.

The *Seal of Solomon* couldn't kill a vampire, but it could sure as hell hurt one.

Before she could rip my throat out, the shadows lifted once more and I heard the fluttering of what sounded like wings. We both froze.

Wings?

A monster such as I'd never encountered before stepped into the moonlight. Its features were more animal than human, the ears pointed like those of a bat and the twin vampire fangs grotesquely elongated. Cadaverous skin that made the other vampires look like devoted sun worshippers stretched across a tall, bony frame. Crimson eyes bored into me as the creature's membranous wings extended from his bony back. The wingspan had to measure about twelve feet, wide enough for the creature to take flight.

Flight over, for example, a downtown skyscraper. Could this winged abomination be the killer who had whisked the demon-worshipping lawyer from his apartment?

In pop culture, vampires could transform into bats and wolves or even mist. Reality was, as always, a tad different.

These creatures were capable of terrible horrors, but shape-shifting wasn't one of them. So what had changed this vampire?

And then the realization hit me.

This master vampire must've fed on the demon, the same demon I had so foolishly liberated. The demonic blood had mutated the vampire in unpredictable ways, giving birth to a terrifying hybrid beast. I had no idea what powers this cross-bred monster possessed, but they had clearly come at a price. Vampires were monsters, but they looked like rock stars and supermodels. This beast had fallen from the ugly tree and taken every branch with it.

As these flippant thoughts whirled through my adrenaline-drenched mind, I wisely kept them to myself. Facing certain death left little room for banter.

"You set the demon free, didn't you?" the winged vampire-demon hybrid said, his voice surprisingly human and refined. It was jarring to hear such a well spoken voice coming from that misshapen maw.

The vampire didn't wait for an answer. "It won't change anything at this point. I drained the demon of all his powers, all his strength. He's nothing but a walking corpse unwilling let go, clinging to a life I took from him, one drop at a time."

As the beast slinked toward me, I feared a similar fate was in store for yours truly. Despite its bulk, the creature managed to move with grace. Another two steps brought it close enough to see a detail the shadows had obscured, and I gasped.

There was a gaping hole where its left eye should be.

I knew of only one vampire who was missing a left eye. Despite a tendency to play things close to the vest, Skulick had shared some information about the vampire who killed his fiancée. One detail stood out. Skulick had shot out the bloodsucker's left eye with a silver bullet before my father finished off the creature.

It couldn't be…Could this be Marek?

Was this the vampire who'd destroyed Skulick's life and set him on his dark monster hunting journey? Had Marek somehow survived my father's blessed bullets all those years ago?

A hideous grin spread across the master vampire's visage. "You know who I am. How is my old friend Skulick? Stuck in that chair of his, a prisoner in his fortress turned prison? How does he manage to go on like that, a bag of broken bones and sagging flesh?"

The vampire-demon drew closer, and I recoiled, natural human revulsion getting the better of me.

"Don't worry, I won't harm you, my frightened little boy. I want you to relay a message to your partner. Tell him that a storm is coming. A storm such as the world has never seen. There will be nothing he can do to stop it. Not him, and not you."

The vampire-demon leaned closer, the sickening stench of the creature turning my stomach.

Fueled by terror, my fist blasted out, the *Seal of Solomon* grazing the vampire-demon's albino skin. The creature didn't even flinch.

From the corner of my eye, I saw Archer lurking in the nearby shadows. She observed us with stony indifference, not a hint of empathy in her icy face. She wouldn't be helping me. I had to admit the truth. The woman I fell in love was gone.

"Your trinkets don't scare me, monster hunter," Marek hissed. His wings flared and knocked me off my feet. Before I could regain my bearings, the winged creature was upon me.

"I know how skeptical Skulick can be, so I need to make sure he knows that I'm back."

I stifled a scream as the vampire's fangs sank into my throat.

And then I felt nothing, my world swept away in a river of blood.

10

The morning sun burned down on me as my eyes snapped open. I lay sprawled on a sidewalk, marinating in a miasma of blood and sweat. As I peered up at my gritty surroundings, I realized I'd been dumped on the loft's doorstep.

They know where we live, was my first thought.

Marek didn't fear us. In fact, he felt so sure of himself and whatever horrible plan he was cooking up, he was willing to provide us with front row seats to the terrible spectacle.

Marek's arrogance gave me hope that Skulick and I might find a chink in the fiend's armor. He had mentioned a storm. What did he mean by that? And could his plan have something to do with the high-rise murder?

My head ached. I had too many questions and not enough caffeine. Not to mention that a vampire had snacked on me—who knows how many pints of blood I'd lost. I was glad to be alive, but my aching bones and the blood-encrusted gash in my throat made it difficult to maintain a positive attitude.

Groggily, I staggered to my feet, my face feeling hot to the touch, feverish almost. Draining me wasn't enough to turn me into a vampire, but like any wound, a bite could become infected if not properly taken care of.

As soon as I lurched into the loft, Skulick's wheelchair buzzed toward me, his disapproving gaze sweeping over me. His expression changed when he realized this wasn't another walk of shame after a night of carousing.

"What happened? Are you alright?"

"Yeah, peachy," I rasped, gingerly touching the wound on my neck.

"How did you get that mark?" my partner asked in a shaky voice, pointing at my neck. The question echoed hollowly in our loft. I'd never seen Skulick so scared before.

"I ran into an old buddy of yours. He sends his regards."

Skulick's' face went white. This wasn't a subject to be making jokes about but I couldn't help myself. My dark sense of humor was a life raft in the ocean of craziness threatening to sweep me away.

I dragged myself over to a nearby mirror and froze. Two twin puncture wounds marred the skin of my neck, one vertical and one horizontal, together forming a cross. Talk about mocking the mythos surrounding vampires. The cross-bite had been Marek's signature. He'd marked all his victims, including Skulick's fiancée, in a similar manner. The bite was the real message here.

"How can Marek be back?" I asked. "I thought you and Dad destroyed him."

"That makes two of us. It's impossible..."

Impossible, unless Dad lied to you, I mused. *Perhaps he wanted you to believe that Marek was out of the picture so you could move on.* "Well, it sure seemed possible last night when he attacked me. Marek survived somehow, and now he's back. And he's planning something terrible."

I quickly brought Skulick up to speed. I expected him to scold me for entering the wrecking yard without backup, but he merely listened to my tale in rapt silence. When I brought up the demon—and how Marek had apparently been warped by feeding on him—Skulick finally interrupted me.

"You set this demon free?"

"It was an accident," I pointed out defensively. "I think Marek had drained the demon to the brink of death and was pretty much done with him."

"And where is this demon now?"

I shrugged. It hurt. "I was going to buy him a beer and catch up on the latest Hell gossip, but I'm afraid he had other plans."

Skulick didn't smile.

"Do you have any idea what Marek meant when he said a storm was approaching?" I asked. "Think he's going to launch an all-out attack against the city?"

Skulick frowned. "A host of vampires can cause a lot damage, but it's not enough to bring down a city of millions. I fear he might be up to something far worse. The fact that he's fed on demon blood changes everything. Your father and I barely defeated Marek thirty years ago, when he was just a vampire, but now..."

Skulick didn't have to finish. We both knew the score–the big bad from my partner's past was back in town and planning on turning our world upside down. We were in for the fight of our lives.

I was just wondering how things could get worse when Skulick asked, "Did you run into Archer?"

I hesitated for a telling beat. I sensed that saving Archer meant almost as much to Skulick as it did to me. Marek had turned his fiancée into a vampire, and my dad had been forced to destroy her. Skulick had never really gotten over it, and I guessed he didn't want me suffer the same fate.

Another thought occurred to me. "The blood in the chalice...it belonged to Marek, didn't it? That's why you held on to it all these years."

Skulick nodded, pensively chewing his lips.

"I never wanted to forget where I came from and why I

was fighting this war," Skulick explained. "If I was to ever doubt the worthiness of our mission, Marek's blood would remind me what it was all about."

It was starting to make sense to me. With Marek's life-force inside of her, Archer had sought out others of her kind. The call of the black blood must have led her to the master vampire himself. Vampires shared a hive mind; Marek could tap into the thoughts of his vampires and draw on their knowledge and memories. I guess that's how he discovered the whereabouts of our base of operation. Archer had led me to Marek, but she had also steered the vampire toward Skulick. In short, Marek now knew everything Archer knew. Our weapons, our defenses—everything.

I was also beginning to understand why Archer hadn't gone on some mad killing spree after escaping from the loft. Marek had protected her from herself, keeping her safely hidden in the shadows, teaching her not just how to hunt but *whom* to target. There were plenty of lost souls out there to feed on. Forgotten people that wouldn't be missed. Marek and his tribe existed on the fringes of society where they would be less likely to draw attention to themselves. At least for now. But that would soon change if Marek was to be believed.

A storm is coming...

"Marek sounds pretty sure of himself," I said. "He's

letting us know that he is up to no good and doesn't seem too worried that we'll be able to stop him."

"His overconfidence is his weakness."

"I'm not the inexperienced homicide detective who faced him thirty years ago."

Skulick's voice simmered with rage. He was a formidable opponent, as knowledgeable about the occult as any man alive. But he was also stuck in a wheelchair. It would be up to me to do the heavy lifting, and that meant I had to get my ass in gear for the upcoming battle.

No more feeling sorry for myself. No more picking fights in alleys. No more drinking.

Okay, *less* drinking.

"We need to figure out what Marek is up to," Skulick said. "I think the demon you set loose might be the key. If anyone does, he would know what Marek has in store for this city."

"So I need to track down this demon, if he hasn't returned to Hell yet…"

"Considering the state he was in, he might be stuck on this plane. You breached Marek's binding circle, but that wouldn't be enough to send the demon back to whatever pit he was conjured from."

I had no idea how Skulick intended to track a single demon in a massive city that sat atop a dimensional rift, but if anyone could crack the problem, it was my partner. His big brain was already going to work as he scanned his computer feeds for any evidence of the creature's whereabouts.

It was around one o'clock, so we still had a few hours of daylight to play catch-up with our new enemy. Marek might have fed on demon blood, but like his undead minions, he was still bound by the rules of his species. These vampires would have to bide their time for at least another five hours until the sun set.

I wondered if Marek and his vampires were still in the junkyard but doubted it. There were hundreds of abandoned buildings in the area where Marek could seek refuge. Skulick was right; tracking down the demon was a better option for now.

Easier said than done.

As Skulick did his thing, I made my way to the vault. The chamber didn't just contain some of the most sinister, insidious occult items in the world. Miracles could be found within–white magic items that had proved essential in our battle with the forces of darkness.

Ignoring the whispering calls all around me, I located a small clay pot containing a creamy gray salve. I liberally applied the salve to my vampire bite wound. Almost immediately, the feverish feelings subsided, a degree of clarity returning to my somewhat erratic thoughts.

Feeling a lot better, I headed for the kitchen. I popped open the fridge, led by my growling stomach. I was desperate for a snack.

Inspecting the meagre contents, I couldn't even recall the last time I went shopping. I settled on leftover burritos from a few days ago. I nuked the burritos and devoured them as if they were a five-star meal. The food helped center me.

I wisely avoided washing them down with a beer. I craved a drink but knew it was a bad idea. I'd never be able to stick with only one once I got started.

It took all my self-discipline to not let my mind wander back to the night at the junkyard. Every time I closed my eyes, Archer's face dominated my thoughts.

I was about to take my last bite when my cell phone rang. It was none other than Benson. The high-rise killer had struck again.

11

Detective Benson had refused to discuss the details of the latest murder on the phone. He had merely provided me with an address.

I still didn't know if there was a connection between the rooftop murders of the demon worshipper and Marek's vampire clan, but my gut said yes. But what purpose could these high-profile crimes serve? And talking about unwanted publicity, why would Marek post the police body-cam video online for the whole world to see? Did he want people to know that vampires were real? And if so, why?

My head was starting to hurt from all the questions. Marek's chilling promise of an impending apocalypse suggested that much bigger things were in store for the Cursed City.

If the murders were part of his plan, then there had to

be some pattern I wasn't seeing yet. It was possible that the killings were less about the victims and more about the placement of the bodies.

I was somewhat familiar with the idea of occult psycho-geography. Humans shape their environment, but the environment also shapes us. If you've ever picked up good or bad vibes from a location, you know what I'm getting at. There are places in the world where supernatural energies are highly concentrated. Some structures can tap into the natural landscape's power by becoming lightning rods for paranormal energy. Geometry, symmetry, design, and occult ritual all play an important role in harnessing such energy.

Had the builders of this apartment tower embedded spells into its foundation? Was Marek hoping to draw on the dormant energy contained within these structures with these killings?

Pushing my gloomy thoughts aside, I parked the Equus Bass and made my way to the skyscraper, which cast a wide shadow over the entire city block. Although it was a sunny day, goosebumps crawled up my arms. For an irrational moment, it almost felt as if the cold was radiating off the hypermodern glass-and-steel monolith. There was something dark and foreboding about this building, and the demon mark on my chest prickled. It was a subtle sensation, a mere hint of paranormal activity, but it convinced me that there was more to this place than met the eye.

I glanced at the plaque in the lobby. Some of the biggest architectural firms in the city rented office space in the structure. Judging by the number of guards and cameras, the security was even tighter than at the last crime scene. Still, it had failed to stop our killer.

Once in the elevator, I raised the collar of my coat, intent on hiding the grisly souvenir Marek had left on my neck. No reason to freak out Benson. A vampire bite mark in the shape of a crucifix isn't exactly a reassuring sight.

As I arrived on the building's blustery rooftop, I was met with an all-too-familiar crime scene. But there were some new nasty surprises waiting for me, too.

Before I could inspect the latest victim, Benson pulled me aside and led me to the edge of the roof. Wind slapped my face, and I instinctively tightened the belt around my flapping coat. I scanned the rooftop for anything that might suggest a mystical connection. Nothing unusual jumped out at me during this cursory inspection. A closer, more careful analysis of the scene would be in order. I suspected occult symbols might be hidden deep within the structure's steel and stone framework, but it would take time to find them.

Benson wordlessly handed me a pair of binoculars.

"Let me guess, you're going to show me the victim's apartment..."

"Not quite," he replied, his voice deadly serious.

He pointed at another tall skyscraper located on the western edge of the city. The buildings faced each other and were nearly the same height, with about a mile between them. For a change, the Cursed City was experiencing a warm, beautiful day. Sunlight glittered against the steel structure framed by an electric blue sky. The weather formed a jarring contrast to the horror of the surreal crime scene.

"Take a look at the roof of the McCormick Building," Benson said.

I frowned but did as requested. The other skyscraper jumped into close view, and I could make out the group of officers gathered on the crowded rooftop. The pit of my stomach tightened as it dawned on me that there must've been two murders.

"Another one?"

Benson nodded gravely.

"Who are the victims?"

"Robert Ibsen and Michael Carver. Ibsen headed up one of the city's top investment firms, Carver was—"

"One of the city's most controversial politicians with his eyes set on a seat in the Senate," I concluded.

When I'm not hunting supernatural fiends, I do crack open a paper from time to time. Or at least I check news alerts on my cell. I wondered if these highly influential men also had ties to the occult like our first victim did.

"Based on forensics, both men were murdered within an hour of each other," Benson said. "The killer only had about sixty minutes to kill the first man and place the body on the roof before trekking crosstown to do it all over again. No way anyone could pull that off..." His shaky voice trailed off.

Poor Benson was still trying to find a rational explanation for these crimes.

"Could there be two killers?" I said.

"Possible, but doubtful considering what the killer did to the two bodies."

I cocked an eyebrow at Benson. "What do you mean?"

"Best if you see for yourself."

We moved away from the ledge and stepped up to the body. Both victims were decapitated. The killer placed the heads next to the bodies, almost as if attempting to hide the damage.

Or as if he had been playing a joke. Vampire humor tended to be bloody.

My mind flashed back to Marek's long, razor-sharp talons. The demon blood had changed him, made him even more monstrous. There was no doubt in my mind that he could easily sever the head of a victim in one fell swoop.

"So he removed the heads," I said, resisting the urge to touch the wound on my neck.

Benson nodded, his face ashen. "It gets crazier. Ibsen's body has Carver's head attached to it and vice versa."

I took a deep gulp, the full horror of the crime sinking in. Marek—I was pretty convinced it had been him—had switched the heads of these two latest victims. There had to be a ritualistic explanation—unless Marek's goal was to kindle terror in the city. If details of the crime got out....

"What the hell is going on here?" Benson said.

I shrugged, at a loss for words. One thing was for certain: occult powers were at work here. Morgal's mark was killing me. The skyscraper was emitting massive bursts paranormal energy. Something terrible had been set in motion by these rooftop murders.

My hope was to find some answers in the victim's apartment downstairs. Benson led me to Ibsen's home, another luxury dwelling with a view to die for. As I combed the extravagant unit for clues, I tried to block out the suspicious glances from the cops. From their perspective, this case was probably freaky enough without having some demon hunter poking around.

I understood their misgivings. They were afraid. Join the club, boys. Facing the nightmares of this world takes its toll on the best of us.

I didn't know exactly what I was looking for. I doubted I would run into another inverted cross or a demonic pattern in the carpet. But if Ibsen was an occultist, there would be signs of his involvement with the darkness.

It took me less than five minutes before I hit pay dirt. My mark began to flare up as I entered the dead man's lavish bedroom. The sensation was most pronounced near the walk-in closet.

Stepping inside, I took in the expensive suits that dominated the space. I wasn't a fashion expert but it was clear to me that Ibsen hadn't been doing his shopping at Walmart. Each piece was tailor made, the material and cut of the highest quality even to my untrained eyes. And considering that I frequently ended up sleeping in my clothes after staggering home drunk or half-dead, my eye was about as untrained as it got.

Despite the wealth on display, the air in the closet had a rank quality, almost as if someone had left a piece of meat to rot. My mark wasn't the only part of me that responded to the presence of great evil. Morgal's wound had changed me, made me more sensitive to the other side. I could see the restless dead, hear the voices of the damned. All of my other senses were capable of tuning into the dark frequency. Right now, my sense of smell was setting off alarm bells. Judging by the placid expression on Benson's face, he wasn't picking up on the foul stench that had assaulted my nostrils.

"What is it?" he asked after taking note of my expression of revulsion.

"There's something bad in here."

Benson took a step back. Holding my breath, I

searched the closet until I located a small cardboard box hidden under a stack of clothing. Fighting back my gag reflex, I peered inside. The stench of decay became overpowering – at least to me. To my surprise, I found a series of photo albums in the box instead of a pile of rotten meat.

I removed the first album, leafed through the pages, and then tossed it aside as if I'd stepped on a live wire. The album was filled with imagery of death and destruction too terrible to describe. Graphic photos of torture, disease and murder filled the album, evil bleeding off every page. A scrapbook from Hell. I expected the other albums in the box to feature even more of this foul depravity. Only a truly deranged mind would collect such snuff.

Or someone who had devoted his life to the cause of evil.

I had a feeling another nasty surprise would be waiting for me half a mile across the city in Carver's apartment. One thing was becoming clear: Marek was targeting human monsters. Followers of the darkness. The question was why.

"Mr. Ibsen had a unique taste in art."

The unfamiliar voice behind me thrust me out of my thoughts. I spun on my heels, coming face to face with the demon I'd released from his prison. He stood in the doorway of the walk-in closet, his sickly form outlined in shadow. He was wearing a black suit, white shirt, and black tie. He almost looked like a Fed. The hollowed-faced visage had filled out a bit since I'd last seen him. How long would it take for the demon to fully regenerate? I didn't plan to wait around and find out.

My hand went for *Hellseeker*. A beat later, I was pointing my magical gun at...Benson. What the hell had happened? The detective stared at me with saucer eyes, stunned by the deadly intent in my face. Most cops underestimated me. They noted my disheveled state, the long coat and hipster beard, and assumed that I was some kind of nutcase or new-age charlatan. They rarely saw me in action battling demons and monsters. They didn't look below the surface to see the monster hunter the forces of darkness had come to fear.

Benson took a step back. "What the hell has gotten into you, Raven?"

The stunned tone of the detective's words brought me back to reality, and I lowered my blessed gun.

"I'm sorry...there are powers at work here..."

I broke off, deciding the less said, the better at this point. Either my mind was playing tricks on me, or the demon was lurking nearby. I suspected the latter to be the case, and that meant the demon's powers were sufficiently restored to bend reality to his unholy will.

I fled the closet, brushing past Benson without uttering another word. I didn't need to see any more proof that these men had been dealing with the dark side—and I definitely didn't want to wait around to see what other tricks the demon had up his sleeve. I surged out of the apartment, homed in on the elevator, and punched the down button. Seconds later, I was on my way to the lobby.

I took a deep breath and wiped the fat drops of sweat from my brow. The building continued to thrum with occult energy. The temperature in the elevator was stifling, a sharp contrast to the unnatural cold which had greeted me outside the building. I was still unbuttoning my coat when the elevator came to a sudden stop and the door split open.

Looming before me was the demon.

As the elevator's fluorescent light played across his bald head, an icy smile crept over his sunken features.

This time I didn't get a chance to draw *Hellseeker*. The demon's bony hand snapped around my wrist and yanked me out of the elevator with inhuman strength. I lost my balance and crumpled to the carpeted hallway floor. By the time, I regained my bearings and my gun was finally out, the demon had once again vanished.

Catching my breath, *Hellseeker* leveled, I peered down the endless, shadow-cloaked hallway. Apartments lined both sides of the corridor. Fear rose in my gut, and I clenched my jaw until I could hear my teeth grinding together.

"Show yourself, damn it! Who and what the hell are you? What game are you playing?"

My voice echoed down the empty corridor. Why had

Morgal's mark failed to sense the demon's presence? Were the building's eldritch vibrations drowning out the demon's presence?

Then I recalled that back in the wrecking yard, I hadn't picked up any supernatural energy from him either. That left only one other explanation. This monster had to be somehow connected to my demonic arch enemy Morgal. Even though my mark responded to supernatural evil, it failed to detect Morgal or those most closely associated with him. And that meant I was in mortal danger.

A stench of rotting eggs and sulfur impregnated the air, making me gag with animal revulsion. The demon was near. Sweat soaked my face. Had someone cranked up the thermostat?

"You have nothing to fear from me," a disembodied voice said from the impenetrable shadows. It required all my self-control to not unload my blessed weapon into the dank hallway.

Patience, I urged myself, *keep it together, wait until he shows himself again.* Wasting ammo when confronting an agent of darkness was never a wise move.

The demon's voice rang down the hallway again, this time emanating from the other direction. *"Do not waste your energy fighting me, Raven. Save your strength for Marek."*

"If you got something to say, show yourself!"

"As you wish," the demon hissed right behind my ear.

His hand shot out, knocking *Hellseeker* out of my grip. My magical weapon went flying.

I whirled.

The demon and I were face-to-face now, less than two feet between us. I still had the *Seal of Solomon*, even thought I doubted it would be able to stop this creature. Weakened as the demon might be, he clearly still had a few tricks up his sleeve.

To my surprise, he scooped up *Hellseeker* and returned the blessed firearm. Smoke curled from his outstretched hand, the flesh sizzling as the magical weapon reacted to his demonic nature. There was a mere flicker of pain on his bony face, quickly suppressed.

"I mean you no harm, monster hunter."

Hesitating, I followed the tendrils of smoke curling from the demon's boiling palm.

"I would appreciate it if you took your gun. I was always more into inflicting pain than experiencing it."

Still expecting it to be a trap, I accepted the gun. The moment the demon let go of *Hellseeker*'s grip, the sizzling stopped and his skin immediately started to regenerate. I had to forcefully resist the urge to bring up my weapon and blow the monster's head off.

Something about the creature's gaze gave me pause. There was a haunted quality to the way he regarded me, a thousand-yard stare I'd caught in my own reflection more than once. This demon had suffered. How long had Marek held him captive, feeding on him until every square inch of his body was covered in bite marks? Was it years? Decades?

"What the hell do you want from me?"

"It appears we have a common enemy. I was hoping we could pool our resources."

The words hung in the air. He had to be joking. Was this creature seriously proposing a partnership between demon and demon hunter?

12

Images of the Cursed City's majestic skyline flickered across the vast bank of monitors that made up Skulick's desk. Various feeds showcased the previous high-rise crime scenes. There was the eighty-story Lennox Building, which dominated the city by sheer size alone. The sleek Art Deco of the Shonji Tower. The gothic majesty of the McCormick Building. These structures had left an indelible impression on the city's skyline even before they became horrific crime scenes.

There was history here, with the oldest structure having risen to the skies at the dawn of the twentieth century. Most people would look at these buildings and see nothing but ordinary skyscrapers. Skulick had done a little research and knew better. History formed a bridge to a world quite different from the present—a world when occultist circles had proliferated and spiritualism had reached new heights. The first World War had wiped out a generation of young men, and people had struggled to come to terms with the loss of so many bright souls. No wonder they had turned to spiritualism, séances and arcane rituals in the hopes of finding the answers they were seeking.

Skulick needed to do more digging into the history of the buildings. There was something strange there, he was sure of it. Unfortunately, Marek's return after all these years made it nearly impossible to focus on the high-rise murder case. Skulick had hoped his research would distract him, but his thoughts kept turning back to the vampire who had destroyed his life.

Marek was back. The nightmare had never truly ended. Perhaps a lack of closure explained why the past continued to have such a hold over him. He'd never been given the satisfaction of destroying his greatest enemy himself, nor had he seen the fiend perish at Richard's hands.

Raven's father had been the one to bring the vamp down, or so he'd claimed. Clearly Marek had found a way to survive, which did raise the question: What had the master vampire been up to for the last three decades? Skulick doubted Marek would have voluntarily kept a low profile for all this time. Somehow the vampire had survived Richard's final attack, but it had taken three decades for him to regenerate himself sufficiently enough to return to the city. The possibility that Richard might've lied to him about Marek's death was too terrible to entertain. No doubt Richard had kept certain things from him over the years, the way he himself shielded Raven from some of the greater horrors. Even so, Skulick refused to believe that his best friend had deceived him about something so important.

The key was to keep his wits about him and not let himself succumb to rampant speculation. There were unanswered questions here, but hopefully the pieces of the puzzle would soon begin to fall in place. The most important part now was figuring out what his old enemy was up to and concentrating his efforts on stopping him.

Marek was cunning and had spared Raven for a good reason. A master of psychological warfare, the vampire master must've predicted that the knowledge of his return would throw Skulick off balance. And it was working.

His attention turned away from the multitude of flickering screens and shifted to the chalice resting on his desk. The origin of the cup was shrouded in mystery. Marek had been working toward something big when Richard had put an end to his bloody reign, and the chalice had been the key to his plan. The cup had held Marek's blood for decades, preserving its unholy power to create more of his kind. What other terrible deeds might it be capable of?

Skulick cursed himself for not getting rid of the chalice earlier. Never in his wildest imagination had he believed it would one day be used to create another monster in Marek's image. In his own way, he was as responsible as Raven for what had happened to Archer. He should have destroyed the chalice and the vampire blood years ago.

With trembling hands, Skulick inspected the contents of the infernal chalice. Raven hadn't used up all of Marek's blood when he'd tried to save Archer. About two ounces of the thick, black liquid remained.

Marek wasn't afraid of him. The demon-vampire clearly didn't fear a broken man trapped in a wheelchair. Skulick knew he was doomed to remain a helpless spectator as Marek's plan unfolded, unless…

His fingers closed around the stem of the chalice. Bile rose in his throat at the sight of the blood and his stomach lurched. The idea of swallowing his greatest enemy's blood, to become a creature he detested with all his heart, filled him with primal revulsion. But there was no other way. He would fight fire with fire, magic with magic.

Blood with blood.

He hadn't told Raven about his plan, or about the angel blood. Marek's return had thrown him for a loop and shifted his priorities. This wasn't a simple rescue mission any longer. This was about avenging Michelle. About stopping Marek. If saving this city came at the price of his own humanity, at the price of his own life, so be it.

There was only enough of the divine essence to save one person from the curse. And that person would be

Archer, not himself. There would be no way to restore his humanity once he swallowed the blood. This was a suicide mission.

Before Skulick could have a change of heart, he snatched the item he'd retrieved from the vault earlier, the *Medal of the Saints*. The protective medallion should shield its wearer from black magic forces. Would donning the medal preserve enough of his humanity for him to resist the corrupting effects of Marek's blood?

Skulick prayed it would.

Mind made up, he downed down the black contents of the chalice, his features distorting with disgust. He let out an explosive cough as the infernal blood crept down his gullet and doubled over.

Pain exploded through every part of his body as the blood spread through his system, infecting his whole being. Skulick was wracked with an agony unlike anything he'd ever experienced in his fifty years on this Earth. The blood roared inside him, burning away all the memories and doubts. Leaving only one all-consuming sensation in their place...

Hunger.

13

I lowered *Hellseeker*, but I didn't take my eyes off the demon. It was eerily quiet in the corridor. No one stepped out of their apartments. Whoever lived in this building either wasn't home or was smart enough not to get caught in the crossfire. I swallowed the bitter lump in my throat and evenly regarded this agent of darkness.

There was only one explanation as to why Morgal's mark hadn't ignited in the presence of true evil. This demon had to be a soldier serving the same demon who'd murdered my parents.

A slap to the face could hardly have hit me harder. And this monster was now asking me to partner with him so we could take revenge against Marek? My first instinct was to dismiss the proposal right out of hand, but another voice inside of me spoke up.

Hear him out, it urged. *Play along for the time being.*

"Who are you? What do you want from me?" I said, struggling to keep emotion out of my voice.

"I have many names, but you can call me Cyon," the demon said, eyes gleaming like black marble. "Marek bound me inside a conjuring circle a year ago so he could drain my blood and steal my powers. But fortunately, you came along."

Fortunate for you, unfortunate for the world.

I gnashed my teeth and said, "You tricked me! I would've never set you free, demon!"

"I have a name, mortal, and I appreciate being addressed by it."

You have one hell of an attitude – pun intended, I thought but held in my tongue.

"We could fight, but I have a feeling in my weakened state you would win, Raven. Marek fed on me and stripped me of most of my powers. I'm but a shadow of who I was. I need your help to defeat him. And you need me if you hope to save your woman."

The last part gave me pause, a chill crawling up my back.

"Go on," I said tightly. Every fiber in my body wanted to grab the demon by the lapels and shake the information out of him.

"It's not too late for Archer, but you must act now."

The muscles in the back of my neck tensed, and I could feel the first stirrings of a headache.

"I'd do anything to save her," I blurted out before I could stop myself.

A cool smile curled the corners of Cyon's lips. I had dealt with enough demons to know that the bald man facing me was but a mask, a flesh suit allowing the monster to blend in among humans. When he smiled, I could see the cracks in the carefully crafted façade.

Cyon took a step toward me and every hair on my body bristled.. I wasn't used to being this close to a demon unless I was firing rounds into it. I didn't like what I saw in those pitiless eyes, but I refused to flinch or look away from the demonic bastard.

"Talk," I said, my voice clipped.

"By now you've figured out that Marek is behind these murders. But I doubt you have any true sense of what's happening."

"And you do?"

There was that grating smile again, and Cyon said, "Of course. The followers of my master, Morgal, designed these buildings. They are lightning rods for demonic energy, conduits of infernal power."

This revelation was lining up with some of my own suspicions, so I said, "Go on."

"When Marek fed on me, he gained my strength as well as all my secrets. The bastard is trying to use Hell's greatest weapon for his own purposes."

That didn't sound reassuring. "Tell me more about this *weapon*."

The demon took a step toward me, his ashen features ghastly in the shadowy corridor. Part of me wanted to take a step back, but I stood my ground. "The three skyscrapers were constructed along a series of ley lines by Norman Mason. They were designed to tap into the landscape's dormant supernatural power."

Mason's name was familiar to me, having come across the man's work many times during my occult studies. Norman Manson was better known as the devil's architect, famous for his ability to weave occult design into his structures. His buildings were known only to a select few, but he had a reputation in certain circles as the Frank Lloyd Wright of occult design.

"Why is Marek targeting demon worshippers?"

"Not demon worshippers, Raven. Demons. To channel the power in these structures, three demons would have to perish."

My mind reeled as I tried to make sense of this latest revelation. "Are you telling me these three murder victims were possessed by demons?"

Cyon nodded. "They were harbored by willing human hosts who allowed them into their hearts and minds."

I considered Cyon's words. The agents of darkness tended to go after the innocent, hoping to corrupt them. It was why children and teenagers made such tempting targets to them. It generally never ended well for the victims, the demons shattering the physical forms of their unwilling hosts. But the three murder victims had been different. The sick bastards had willingly given their physical bodies over to these beasts from Hell.

"Thesse three demons were willing to sacrifice themselves to activate the building's power?"

Cyon snorted. "Sacrificial fools."

Clearly Cyon didn't approve of the plan.

"How did Hell intend on channeling this the building's power?"

"It was supposed to fuel a final ritual."

I hated to ask, but it needed to be said. "What sort of ritual?"

"One that would corrupt tens of thousands."

My mind was spinning. "What are you talking about?"

"Mass possession," Cyon explained. "Imagine every sinner in this city falling under the spell of Morgal. A city of millions would devour itself, falling into chaos and despair, signaling that a new age of evil was upon the world."

Damn. That was...not good. I raked a hand through my hair, trying to wrap my head around the full extent of this infernal plot.

Only one question remained. How did Marek fit into this? If the master vampire was sacrificing these demons, did it mean he was taking over Hell's ritual somehow, twisting it to his own dark objectives?

I was reminded of Marek's cryptic words: *A storm is coming.* A vampire blood rite was troublesome enough on its own, but with the three buildings' dark power amplifying the range and scope of the ritual...

"Marek isn't looking to trigger mass possession," Cyon said, interrupting my fatalistic train of thought. "He seeks to unleash a vampiric plague such as the world hasn't experienced since the Dark Ages."

Before my mind's eye, I saw thousands of city dwellers turning into ravenous bloodsuckers. I shuddered at the grisly image.

"Together we can stop Marek and save this city. Isn't that what you do, demon hunter? Save people from the nightmares?" Cyon's expression veered between mockery and amusement.

I glared at him. "How do I know you won't set the original ritual in motion once we stop Marek?"

"You don't." The demon flashed me a sarcastic grin. It almost felt like the emaciated bastard was enjoying himself.

"Sorry, but you're not selling me on this partnership, buddy. Last time I ran into you, you didn't seem to have any qualms about leaving me behind for Marek to finish off."

Cyon's smile shrank, the expression on his skull-like

features darkening. "I was disoriented, drained to the brink of death, and consumed with a hunger for freedom. Getting out of there after being Marek's prisoner for so long was all that mattered to me."

"You serve the archdemon who murdered my parents," I said.

"Nowadays I serve no master but myself." The playful, mocking tone was gone from Cyon's voice, replaced with a chilly undercurrent of danger. "Morgal turned his back on me once Marek trapped me in his binding circle. I begged my master to save me, but my pleas went unheard. Morgal could have easily interfered on my behalf, yet he didn't. You want to know why, mortal? By allowing myself to be captured by a vampire, my master deemed me unworthy."

I nodded. The lords of darkness didn't look kindly upon failure.

"That day I vowed I'd do everything in my power to stop my former master if I was to somehow escape."

The demon's voice dripped with rage. I had a feeling Cyon wasn't telling me the full story, but his hatred for both Marek and Morgal was genuine.

I was tempted to believe Cyon. After all, the demon had the inside track when it came to Marek. But I'd been battling the forces of darkness long enough to know that demons, even those wronged by their master, weren't to be trusted.

The Devil was known as the Prince of Lies for a good

reason. His minions were cut from the same cloth. Who knew what game this monster might be playing? Sure, he wanted revenge—but what would happen once the master vampire was out of the picture? The moment I turned my back on him, odds were high he'd double cross me. Delivering me to Morgal would definitely get him back in the archdemon's good graces. I refused to take that chance.

"Sorry, bud, but I don't work with the enemy."

"How does the old saying go again? The enemy of my enemy is my friend, monster hunter."

Good point. The persuasive bastard sure didn't like to give up. But I could be stubborn too.

"Morgal murdered my family!" I snapped. "I've seen over and over again what your kind is capable of."

"I assume that means you won't help me."

"You're smarter than you look."

"Perhaps you'll change your mind as the night approaches."

The sudden sound of a lock being opened made me tighten my grip on *Hellseeker*. A beat later, a tall Asian man emerged from his apartment. He gaped at me when he spotted the green glowing gun in my hand and slammed the door shut. Smart guy. By the time I shifted my attention back to Cyon, the demon had vanished into thin air. Great.

I checked my watch and choked back a surprised gasp. Hours had passed during my conversation with the demon. Once more, the monster' presence had warped space and time. Dammit! It would be dark within less than an hour. So much for having the whole afternoon to plan a counterattack against Marek. I suspected Cyon had held me here for so long to increase the odds of me joining forces with him.

Still wondering if I'd made a terrible mistake by refusing this alliance with Cyon, I made my way out of the building. Was going up against Marek and his army of vampires on my own the smartest move?

I didn't need to team up with some demon to take down Marek. You want to know why? I already had a partner. If anyone knew how to deal with Marek, it would be Skulick.

Reassured by this thought, I climbed into my muscle car and fired up the engine. High above, the supernaturally charged building cast its ominous shadow over the Cursed City. It felt like a harbinger of darker things to come.

14

The night belongs to me, Skulick thought as he sprinted across a series of dark rooftops like some Parkour artist on steroids. As he reached the edge of the roof, he didn't pay attention to the six-story drop. Nor did he slow down. Instead he fearlessly launched himself into the air, confident of clearing the twenty-five-foot gap. Air whistled through his hair as the neighboring rooftop jumped into view. Seconds later, his feet were on solid ground again. Never slowing down, he kept on moving through the darkness.

His formerly shattered body hummed with strength and energy. After spending a long year trapped in a wheelchair, being able to use his legs again felt more amazing than he could ever have imagined. A dark joy filled his heart—and he hated himself for it.

Even though he was technically undead now, he felt more alive than ever. His newly enhanced senses were on fire, the darkness alive with a myriad of new sights and sounds. Moonlight pulsed around him, revealing colors and textures beyond human senses. He heard a couple making love in an apartment across the street, a small child crying out in the unit two buildings down from him, a homeless man riffling through a dumpster on the streets below. Every sight and sound told its own story, providing the voyeuristic rush of peeking into another world.

At first, Skulick had feared he might succumb to sensory overload. Somehow he was not only able to absorb all the new impressions bombarding him from every direction, but he craved more of them. He wanted to devour every sensation, to drink in every minute detail of the night. Marek's blood in his veins had turned him into a god.

A monster, he corrected himself. *And what you really want to drink is blood.*

Despite wearing the *Medal of the Saints*, he was struggling to cling to the memory of the man he once was. Only his hatred for Marek kept him from succumbing to the vampire blood's dark call—the need to feed, to sink his fangs into living flesh was overpowering. He had embraced the darkness to slay the vampire who'd stolen his life, not to become a soulless monster himself.

The wooden stake in his hand felt rough to the touch, and his vampire nature recoiled from its power. Adorned with a series of glyphs, it was purported to have been carved from the wood of the cross that Jesus had died on. The blessed stake was known as the *Bloodslayer*, and Skulick planned to use it first against Marek before driving it into his own heart.

Skulick hurtled through the air once more, landing on the next rooftop. He maintained his grueling pace for a few more seconds before finally slowing down. He wasn't tired. He'd simply reached his destination.

Up ahead, a few hundred feet beyond his current position, the wrecking yard awaited him. The blood roaring through his veins had steered him to the place where Raven had first run into his old foe. Marek hadn't even deemed them enough of a threat to move his nest to another location.

I'm coming for you, you cocky bastard, Skulick thought, his emotions cresting. Marek's overconfidence would be his undoing.

Skulick dove off the building. He dropped with superhuman grace and landed on the street. Picking up his pace again, he surged toward the six-foot chain-link fence and leapt over the barrier without hesitation. Moments later he was inside the junkyard, his eyes combing the stark surroundings. A post-apocalyptic wasteland of rotting machinery stretched out in all directions. The junkyard seemed deserted, but Skulick knew better. Marek's blood had led him to this place for a reason. The demon-vampire and his unholy tribe were here.

Fingers clutched tightly around the *Bloodslayer,* Skulick dove into the dark car cemetery.

Moving swiftly, Skulick pulled the hood of his dark jacket over his head and edged deeper into the maze of broken cars. The plan was to infiltrate the vampire tribe and get close enough to Marek to launch an attack before the demon-vampire knew what hit him. Judging by what Raven had told him, Marek's new crew consisted of a ragtag group of runaways, homeless people, and other forsaken souls. Newly made vamps consumed by ravenous, animalistic needs, which left little room for strategic thinking. Without Marek's guidance, they could easily be taken out one by one. Skulick wanted Marek's followers to see their master go down. Cut off the head of the viper and the body will soon follow—a sound philosophy in battle.

A sound made Skulick whirl.

Lurking behind a gutted Jeep was a lonesome figure sporting a ragged hoodie. More of the urban spooks quickly joined the first vampire. The pale figures slipped from the mountains of jagged steel and gathered in the clearing, almost as if they were following some silent summoning call.

The call of the night, Skulick thought. *The call of my master's blood.*

He froze, horrified by his own thoughts. *Their master*, he desperately corrected himself. *Not mine.*

Despite the protective properties of the *Medal of the Saints*, he could feel Marek's call stirring inside him. He was gripped by visions of himself sinking his teeth into the living, feasting on their hot blood.

No! Clenching his jaw, he shook off the horrible thoughts threatening to take hold of him. *Focus on the mission.*

His enhanced senses combed the darkness, searching for Marek as his tribe filled the wrecking yard. One by one, more silhouettes peeled away from the metallic refuse, the ghostly pallor of their faces enhanced by the moonlight. Skulick counted at least twenty. Could he pull this off without the undead horde tearing him apart first? He itched to use the magical stake that he kept hidden under his over-sized hoodie.

Be patient, he urged himself. *Stay calm. Your chance to strike will come all too soon.*

The gang of vampires ignored him, apparently seeing him as one of their own. Which, all things considered, wasn't that far off the mark. Analyzing the movement of the group, Skulick realized they were gathering around an imposing car crusher. The towering compactor jutted from the landscape of ravaged and razed cars like a cathedral devoted to some post-apocalyptic god. The air crackled with anticipation. A beat later, a figure appeared atop the car crusher.

Skulick took a step closer and narrowed his eyes.

If Skulick had still been alive, his breath would have caught in his throat. He had steeled himself for this moment, played it in his mind's eye many times, but the reality still hit him hard. It was the monster who had murdered his fiancée. Who had taken everything from him.

Raven had described Marek as a bat-like creature, horribly twisted by the demon blood he had consumed, but the figure looming above the crowd now resembled the Marek of his nightmares. Handsome, seductive, cruel. Longish jet-black hair framed perfectly chiseled ivory features. Only the missing eye blemished his face. It seemed Marek still possessed the ability to shift back and forth between his old visage and his new, more monstrous self.

On some level it would have been easier to face a winged monstrosity than the vampire who had haunted him for all these years. Over the last three decades, Skulick had faced his share of beasts. He didn't fear monsters, but the sight of that familiar, coldly cruel face sent a pang of fear through his heart.

Skulick's fingers whitened around the stake. He pushed the memories of his fiancée out of his mind and instead focused on visualizing himself driving the *Bloodslayer* through Marek's undead heart.

The time had come to challenge his love's murderer to a duel to the death. A part of him still wondered how Marek had survived Richard's attack thirty years earlier, but his hatred far outweighed his curiosity. Why did it matter? They'd both be dead soon. All Skulick had time for was vengeance.

Determined, Skulick drew closer.

"My children, the time has come to reveal ourselves to this city."

Marek's seductive voice rang through the night, exuding power and confidence. Skulick fought back the irrational impulse to throw down the stake and tear off his protective medallion so he could join the ranks of Marek's army.

Skulick gritted his teeth, his determination fraying. The call of Marek's blood threatened his resolve. An image of Michelle's face, lovely and laughing, filled his mind. He would not fail her now, not again.

Skulick willed himself forward. To his growing horror, he struggled to tap into the hatred that had fueled his mission for all these decades. Each step became an excruciating exercise, almost as if the terrain was holding him back. The blood's power was growing stronger as he zeroed in on Marek.

"We have dwelled in the dark corners of the world for

far too long, hiding in the shadows when we should be ruling this world," Marek said. "No one will stop us from taking our rightful place."

Marek's gaze locked on Skulick, and he realized the jig was up.

"Not even you, Detective Skulick!"

Skulick froze in place, sensing the full attention of the tribe of vampires turning toward him.

"It's so nice for you to join us," Marek said. There was no fear in the demon-vampire's voice, no sense of alarm.

The vampires closed in, radiating a sense of coiled menace. One word from their master, and this horde would be on him like vultures on carrion. He could see their nails lengthening into razor-like talons.

"Marek," Skulick growled.

"Did you believe you could sneak up on me with my blood in your veins?"

Skulick clenched his jaw. *This is it!*

One hand whipped out a high-intensity UV light he had brought along and spun it at the vamps encircling him. The blinding light fell across their albino features, sizzling skin.

As the howls of the blistering vampires filled the night, Skulick launched himself at the car crusher. He landed on top of the compactor. Moving like a machine, he spun the UV light toward the master-vampire, and the creature emitted a roar of agony. His other hand drew the *Bloodslayer* and spun toward his arch-nemesis.

Marek backed off, the magical stake missing him by inches. They looked at each – into each other – mere feet between them. Marek's remaining inhuman eye flashed with fury.

An instant later, the demon-vampire was upon him, attacking with ferocious, manic energy. The claws slashed Skulick's hoodie, shredding fabric and slicing the flesh below. Black blood oozed from the wound, and Skulick stifled a scream as he stumbled back. Below them the congregation of vampires watched the battle in hushed silence.

"I've waited for this a long time, detective," Marek said.

"Thirty years," Skulick replied. He tried to maneuver *Bloodslayer* into position. The vampire seemed unconcerned, possibly thinking it was an ordinary stake. Well, Skulick planned to teach him otherwise. "Strange how it took a monster to create a monster hunter," Marek continued. "Tell me, Skulick, what is the last thing you see when you close your eyes at night? Is it your dead lover, or is it me draining the last drop of life from her?"

Marek's words were meant to throw him off, make him lose his cool so he would do something stupid. And goddamnit, it was working. Even though he tried to block out the taunts, he could feel rage sweeping all rational thoughts aside. Marek was getting to him. He had to finish the bastard off fast.

With renewed determination surging through him, Skulick leaped at the master-vampire. He dodged two ferocious thrusts from Marek's talons, then came in low and rammed his blessed stake into the undead bastard.

For a split second, the world froze. He could see the surging mob below the car crusher grow still, felt the shock ripple through the crowd of hooded followers.

He'd done it.

He'd managed to put an end to the ancient undead evil.

Skulick expected the demon-vampire's face to shrivel up and turn to ash, as lesser vampires did when staked, but instead the fiend's lips curled up into a diabolical smile. Before Skulick could react, the demon-vampire's clawed hand snapped around Skulick's grip on the stake. The tendons and muscles on his forearm thickened, growing more powerful but also misshapen. One of the little bones in Skulick's hand snapped under the force of the vampire's grip.

He looked down at the stake. The *Bloodslayer* should have destroyed Marek.

Adrenalized by a dark energy, Marek's skin thickened, forming a kind of reptilian flesh armor, becoming even more demonic in appearance. The face caved in, elongating, as rows of pointed teeth joined the vampire fangs. The skin grew mottled and reptilian, a series of horns erupting from the skull. And finally, the shoulders cracked and buckled, and giant, bat-like wings exploded from the master vampire's back. As the wings unfurled, they blocked out the moonlight above.

It dawned on Skulick that he'd made a terrible miscalculation. Raven had told him that the monster he now faced wasn't merely a vampire any longer but something different.

Something more.

And that meant the rules for destroying Marek had changed.

A peal of monstrous laughter erupted from the demon-vampire as he yanked out the stake and cast it aside. The blessed wood dripped black blood as it clattered on the ground fifteen feet below the crusher.

Then one of the massive wings slammed into Skulick and swept him off the crusher.

He crashed to the ground, the impact sending up plumes of dust. Before Skulick could scramble back to his feet, Marek's giant winged shadow engulfed him.

Skulick tried to back away, but the tribe of vampires kept him hemmed in. There was nowhere to go.

"I will rule this city," Marek promised. He leaned closer and added, "And you, my dear detective, will stand by my side as my blood rains down the sky and wipes this place clean of the human scourge."

With these words, Marek tore the *Medal of the Saints* off Skulick's neck, and the world transformed into a place of inhuman hunger and darkness.

15

Night had already fallen by the time I arrived back at the loft. My stomach churned with anxiety. Marek and his vampires were out there somewhere, gearing up for the final stage of the blood ritual.

A storm is coming.

I struggled to push my fatalistic thoughts aside and maintain a positive outlook on the situation, but my sense of impending dread increased the moment I set foot in the loft. I knew immediately something was terribly wrong. Someone had turned off the computer screens on Skulick's desk.

Impossible.

My partner never shut off his lifeline to the outside world, not even when he was sleeping. The flickering screens never went dark. At least not until this moment.

I surged toward the desk and stopped dead in my tracks. An empty wheelchair sat next to the dark monitors. I don't know for how long I stood there, staring at the abandoned chair with a dumbfounded expression plastered across my face. Where was my partner? It wasn't like he could get up and walk away…

My gaze fell across the chalice resting on the floor. It was empty.

Oh no…

He'd done it. Skulick had taken the blood. There was a mad logic to it, emphasis on "mad." I vividly recalled how shaken Skulick had been when he learned about Marek's return. Desperate times call for desperate measures and all that. My partner had been this city's silent guardian for years, watching over it best he could. But this was one fight he would refuse to observe from behind the safety of his command desk. He'd sacrificed everything to get a chance at revenge. To stop the master vampire. Dammit, I should have seen this coming.

I held up the cup to the light, confirming that the dark liquid had been drained from it. Only a few drops remained. My heart sank. History was repeating itself. Once again, it appeared that I'd lost another person I cared deeply about. First my parents, then Archer, and now Skulick.

Blood rushed in my ears, and I craved a drink. Maybe just one to steady my nerves. Losing my partner to the wheelchair less than a year ago had been a devastating blow. But as time had passed, I'd adjusted. Skulick might not have been by my side any longer when I battled the horrors of this city, but he was always a phone call away. A steady, guiding presence in my life. In a way, Archer had taken his place, at least in the field but now I was utterly alone.

A sudden wave of anger washed over me. How could Skulick have been so foolish? Did he believe he could resist the call of the dark blood? Hadn't he learned anything from what had happened to Archer? Becoming a vampire wasn't the way to defeat Marek. God, he had played in the monster's hands. My lips trembled as I balled my fists in helpless anger, fury turning into paralyzing sadness. And that's when my gaze landed on the iPad sitting next to the black monitors. A sticky note was attached to its screen. It read PLAY ME.

Another surprise was waiting for me next to the iPad. A cross-shaped bottle filled with what appeared to be liquid energy. I shielded my gaze, and wondered what I was looking at. My gut told me Skulick's message might hold the answers.

My sense of dread increased as I turned on the device. The screen lit up and Skulick appeared on the screen. His face looked ashen, haunted yet determined. A warrior preparing himself for the final battle.

"*If you're watching this, Raven, you know what I was*

forced to do. Believe me when tell you that this was one the hardest decisions I have ever had to make."

The most foolish one, I thought as I fought back my rising anger.

"My heart is heavy but I have no choice. I hope in time you will be able to understand my decision. I'm so sorry Raven, but there was no other way. I must face this monster and put an end to Marek once and for all. I promise you that as soon as I defeat Marek, I will turn the stake on myself. You won't have to come after me."

"Damn it, Skulick," I growled.

Onscreen, he pointed to a hammered gold disc hanging from a leather cord around his neck. "I'm wearing the *Medal of the Saints* in the hopes that it will protect me from the blood's demonic influence long enough to complete my task. I've also taken the *Bloodslayer* from the vault." He paused, his tired but determined eyes seeming to meet mine. *"Raven, there's one more thing I need to tell you. I believe I've found a cure for vampirism. Angel blood is the one substance that might be powerful enough to reverse the effects and restore a vampire to humanity. I managed to track down a small vial of it through my contacts."*

My heart was pounding by now, my fingers gripping the iPad so hard I was afraid I might break it before the video finished. A cure? Could it be possible?

"There is only enough angel blood to save Detective Archer," Skulick continued. *"More than anyone, I know what*

you must be going through and how hard the last month must've been. I'm an old, broken-down demon hunter, my boy. I've reached the end of my life, but you still have decades ahead. Save the woman you love. Do what I couldn't. I waited thirty years for this moment. The time has come for me to finish Marek for good."

The video was almost over, mere seconds remaining. I couldn't bear to keep watching, but I also couldn't tear my gaze from the screen.

"I've seen you go from a frightened little boy to the man you are today. And even though I bust your chops from time to time, I couldn't be prouder of the man you've become. I never had children of my own, but if I had..."

I killed the video and forcefully wiped away a tear from my eye. I did what I always did when my emotions boiled over: I turned the pain into anger.

"What a crock of shit, old man! We are supposed to be a team, god damn it! You don't go off drinking vampire blood without at least talking to me first."

Just like I should have talked to him before I went to the wrecking yard. I gnashed my teeth, considering my options. There had to be a way out of this. I just needed to think...

My cell chirped. The incoming Facetime message was from none other than my partner. Taking a deep breath, I answered the call and my blood turned to ice. The crazed beast glaring back at me couldn't be Skulick. It shared little in common with the calm, calculating demon hunter I knew. The skin was marble, the eyes slitted and tinted scarlet. And then there were the fangs.

My breath hitched. Seeing him like this was worse than anything I could have imagined.

But wait. If Skulick had already gone over to the dark side, consumed by blood lust, then who was sending me the video?

Heavy silver chains bound my mentor. The camera pulled back, revealing a large crane inside the by now familiar wrecking yard. A cable extended from the arm of the crane, one hooked end attached to Skulick's shackled form.

A pneumatic hiss sounded, and the crane lifted Skulick's writhing form into the air. The camera pulled further back until I only saw a small shape struggling twenty feet off the ground.

An all-too-familiar voice spoke from offscreen. "Right now, Detective Skulick may be feeling a little uncomfortable. But things will get a lot worse once the sun rises. You've destroyed enough of us to know what's in store for your partner. And once I'm done with him, dear little Archer will be next."

Marek's monstrous presence filled the phone's screen as he turned it to face him. He held up the stake known as the *Bloodslayer*, and despair gripped me. It dawned on me that Marek had wanted this from the start. That's why I had been spared—to draw Skulick into a direct confrontation with the master vampire. Assuming that Marek had also gotten his hands on the *Medal of Saints*, the bastard now had two of our most powerful defenses against the undead.

"What do you want from me?" I growled.

"I want what is rightfully mine. Bring me the chalice before sunrise, or the people you care most about will perish in a fiery blaze."

The cell's screen went dark. I don't know for how long I just stood there, staring into space. Eventually, I picked up the chalice. Moonlight seeped in from the skylight above and played across its intricately adorned surface. Only a few drops of the master vampire's blood remained in the cup.

I couldn't give it to him. I couldn't hand Marek a relic that would allow him to turn thousands of innocent people into bloodthirsty monsters. Neither Skulick nor Archer would want that. But I couldn't let my friends die either.

Besides refusing to deliver the chalice would not be the end of it. Marek would try to take the artifact by force. Despite our base's protective wards and runes, I held no illusion that the loft was a safe haven. Somehow, Marek would find a way to get what he wanted.

My grip tightened around the cup in my hand and it

required all my will power not to hurl the cursed relic out of the window.

God, how I wished I had never laid eyes on the damn thing. I wished I could go back in time and stop myself from ever entering the vault on that fateful night. One bad decision had set the current chain of events in motion. No matter what I did now, the two people I cared about the most in this world were doomed.

A wailing alarm cut through the loft. Someone was attempting to breach our perimeter.

That was quick, I thought, dragging my mind back to the present.

Had Marek's phone call been nothing but an elaborate distraction? Were the members of his unholy clan already here, ready to burst into our base and take what they wanted by force?

I moved toward Skulick's desk and switched on the bank of CCTV monitors. Eight cams offered a comprehensive view of the surrounding streets and various entrance points to the loft. I almost let out a sigh of relief when I spotted the intruder who had set off the screeching alarm. It was Cyon.

I never thought I would be in such dire straits that I'd be happy to see a demon on my doorstep.

He looked up at the camera as if he knew I was watching him. Who was I kidding? Of course he knew. I switched on the audio. "What are you doing here?"

"I thought you might finally be ready to reconsider my offer. I can help you stop Marek, Raven, and save your friends."

I considered Cyon's offer. And that's when a crazy idea occurred to me. There might be a way to turn the table on Marek. It would be risky but it was my best shot at defeating the vampire demon and saving my friends. But I would need help to pull this off.

The help of a demon.

"Let's talk" I said.

As Cyon flashed me a smile through the surveillance camera, I couldn't help but feel like I was about to make a deal with the devil himself.

16

A cold wind whipped down the abandoned city streets as I hurtled through the night on my black Ducati. The promise of imminent rainfall filled the air. I'd traded my trench coat for a motorcycle jacket, but it felt strange to go into battle without my usual armor. I was ready to face Marek. Cyon and I had hashed out a plan that might be crazy enough to work. Only time would tell.

Lightning split the sky, illuminating the wrecking yard up ahead. Stacks of cars grew visible behind the chain link fence, the Cursed City's imposing skyline glittering in the near distance.

From this angle, I could make out two of the occult skyscrapers where the demons had been sacrificed. The tall towers now glowed with a spectral, pulsating light. This unnatural glow was only visible to people with a sixth sense like myself. Judging by the many new messages in my voice mail, most of my psychic friends in the city had picked up on the activity too.

Joe Cormac, who had helped me a few weeks earlier, was among the callers. I had barely spoken with the Gulf War vet turned ghost hunter since my battle with Engelman's spirit at Blackwell Penitentiary. I promised myself to call him back—if I should be lucky enough to survive the night.

I wasn't enthusiastic about my chances. Especially with Cyon as my only backup.

As my bike screamed through the open front gate, I couldn't help but notice how much had changed in the last twenty-four hours. There was no more sneaking around. Marek knew I was coming, the open gate a clear invitation to join the party. The bag with the chalice rested heavily against my body. It felt like at least fifty pounds of dead weight was digging into my shoulder.

Weirdly enough, the cup seemed to have grown heavier as I drew closer to the wrecking yard. All too soon the relic would be reunited with its dark master. Thinking of the horrors Marek hoped to unleash with the help of the chalice made me shiver. Above the glittering metropolis, forks of lightning illuminated the approaching cloud bank.

A storm was closing in, just as Marek had promised.

I slowed my approach as my bike zeroed in on the

center of the junkyard. Moving shadows and whispers filled the darkness. A circle of hooded figures had gathered around the massive, temple-like car crusher. Flashing lightning revealed Marek's winged, gargoyle-like form atop the compactor. I didn't have to see Marek's monstrous features to feel his sense of triumph. The son of the monster hunter who'd tried to kill him thirty years earlier was about to hand him the key to the vampire apocalypse.

My cycle sputtered to a halt, and I removed my helmet. Icy air bit my face as the storm gathered strength above us. I wondered if the weather was the result of the black magic pulsing off the skyscrapers. Bursts of paranormal energy were already leaking into the atmosphere.

Scanning the area, I found my partner. He still hung from a steel cable attached to a nearby crane, chains wrapped around his dangling form. My heart sank as my gaze found his face. Little of the man who had been like a father to me remained. In place of Skulick's cool intellect, there was only animalistic, snarling hunger.

Shaken, my grip tightened around the duffel bag. Taking a deep, steadying breath, I eyed the congregation of vampires. Was I a fool for giving Marek the magical cup? Was I about to hand over the launch codes to Hell's most dangerous weapon? But looking up at Skulick's struggling form reminded me why I was here. And I did have plan. A crazy plan but a plan nonetheless. There was still a chance of saving the people I cared about the most, and I planned to seize it.

With a renewed sense of determination, I advanced toward the crusher, the bag with the chalice held high.

Marek's voice rose over the wind. "Son of Richard, have you brought the cup?"

I answered the question by snapping open the satchel and removing the golden grail. I held it up high, the relic bathed in moonlight and lightning, allowing all the vampires gathered around to see it. A murmur of excitement passed through the crowd.

Unable to control his eagerness, Marek dove from the crusher and swooped toward me, wings extended. A beat later, his massive form slammed into the ground before me, the impact of his landing sending up clouds of dust. I stifled a cough, unwilling to show any form of weakness in front of the vampire-demon hybrid.

"Hand me what is rightfully mine," Marek hissed.

There was one last beat of hesitation before I handed the vampire-demon the cup.. Marek regarded me coolly.

"Your father tried to kill me thirty years ago. But I managed to outlive him." The monstrous creature took a step toward me. "You want to know what my greatest regret is? That I didn't get to kill him myself. I will have to settle for you, his son."

I stood my ground. "My father believed he killed you thirty years ago. How did you survive?"

Instead of providing a verbal answer, Marek's clawed hand brushed against me. A primal sensation of revulsion filled my entire being. Then, the world around me changed in a metaphysical flash.

I found myself on a bridge shrouded in fog, running for my life. Despite my punishing pace, my heart wasn't pounding in my chest. In fact, there was no heartbeat. I wasn't breathing, either. Blood oozed from my chest. Black blood. I took note at the ghostly pallor of my hands before I shifted my attention to the oncoming footsteps. A figure was tearing after me, lethal determination in his eyes. He was wearing a trench coat, a green glowing pistol in his right hand. *Hellseeker*, I realized. For a split second, I felt like I was looking into a mirror. Then it dawned on me. This was my dad, and that could only mean...

The brief physical contact with the vampire-demon had triggered a vision of the past. Of course. I was reliving Marek's encounter with my father thirty years ago. I was inside his memory, a silent spectator of the past. I'd experienced something similar before, when a maddened ghost had trapped me in the memories of her death.

The world slowed to a crawl as my father fired at me... no, at Marek. Bullets tore into me, a pain beyond anything I'd ever experienced. I saw my limbs shrivel up and wither as I was propelled by the impact against the bridge's steel railing.

In an act of desperation, I flung myself over the side. I

fell for what seemed like an eternity, the eighty feet between the bridge and the river below stretching out endlessly. My flailing body cut through the night, trailing fire and ash.

When I hit the choppy water, the impact rattled every bone in my body. The agony triggered by the blessed bullets consumed my nerve endings. The freezing water enveloped me, and the world above vanished.

The surface grew dimmer as my dying body sank to the bottom of the river in a cloud of black blood. I was gravely wounded but still clinging to life. It would have been easy to let the darkness swallow me whole, but something stopped me from letting go.

Hatred.

Hatred for the two brazen mortals who'd hunted me down like prey. By the time reached the bottom, I was a cadaverous shadow of my former self...yet I was still alive. I refused to die.

Years passed.

Decades.

Time ceased to have meaning. But the hatred continued to burn bright.

And then one day...

A violent ripple above me drew my attention, followed by a rush of movement.

A shape shot toward me through the dark depths of the river. It was a woman. She was in bad shape, her heartbeat faint. Already near death from the impact of the fall. I sensed desperation and fear in her dying mind. She had willingly hurled herself off the bridge in the hopes of ending her pathetic existence. But her suicide attempt hadn't been completely successful. Even though her soul craved oblivion, her body still clung to life.

She wanted to die, and I wanted to live. Soon, both our wishes would come true.

She was so close. As long as her heart hammered, pumping blood through her dying system, I could still feed on her.

I sprang like a cobra, my skeletal hand closing around her neck. There was a moment of horror as her eyes snapped open. I could hear her thoughts. She already believed herself to be dead. Believed me to be a demon greeting her on her way to Hell. Emotions cascaded through her mind. Guilt, regret, and terror. Too late for second thoughts...

My fangs found the soft skin of her throat, the life pulsating within it. And then the water turned red... and pain gave way to ecstasy as I fed for the first time in decades. Life returned to my shriveled limbs. I had waited, conserved my energy, allowed myself to heal. I was finally ready to return to the surface. Return to the world. And as the last drop of life left the woman's body and her eyes grew dull, I could feel the old power surging through me.

I was still too weak to reveal myself to my enemies. I

would keep feeding, growing stronger and gathering a tribe. The centuries had taught me the value of patience. What was one more year after spending decades at the bottom of the river?

I was back.

Let the world beware.

I recoiled from Marek, my body shaking as if I'd been doused with freezing cold water. The memory had been so raw and vivid. For a brief moment, I'd become Marek. I'd experienced the world through the monster's mind.

"Now you finally understand my pain, Raven," he said knowingly. "My rage. My need for vengeance."

Lightning forked, splitting the sky from one end to another, filling the air with electricity. The hungry anticipation in the crowd of vampires was growing.

Wary, spent from the flashback Marek had shared with me, I took a step back. My gaze combed the crowd of vampire onlookers and found the person I was looking for. Archer met my questing gaze with icy indifference. The two people I cared about the most in the world were less than twenty feet away from me, yet I'd never felt so alone in my life. Even when my parents had died, there had been Skulick's soothing presence. Not any longer.

Time to grow up, kid.

My attention turned back to Marek. I watched in silent horror as he slashed his own wrists. Black blood seeped from the pale flesh, dripping into the chalice. Why hadn't he struck me down yet? After all, my father had nearly condemned him to a watery grave. Only one explanation could explain my stay of execution. The master vampire wanted me to witness his greatest triumph before he finished me off. Simply striking me down would be way too fast. Marek wanted to draw out my pain, deepen my sense of defeat. I balled my hands into fists, helplessness turning into simmering rage.

Another bolt of sizzling electricity split the darkness, strobing Marek in its eerie glow. The vampire-demon hybrid uttered a series of words in a language I've never encountered before as he raised the chalice toward the sky.

I remembered Skulick mentioning the existence of an ancient vampire tongue. It had been spoken centuries in the past when vampires ruled certain medieval kingdoms in Eastern Europe. Records of these terrible times were fragmented, believed to be myths and and shrouded in mystery. Whatever ritual Marek was setting into motion now, must have been born during that horrible age of darkness.

I struggled to fight back my growing doubts. How could I hope to defeat this monster with only a broken demon in my corner?

A clap of thunder shattered the silence as lightning struck the chalice.

At the exact same moment, more bolts speared the night. They extended like electrical tentacles toward the occult skyscrapers, connecting the three buildings with the chalice. Marek's vampiric blood had become part of the flow of paranormal energy.

Hell's super-weapon was active.

Above us, the lightning intensified, and the churning black storm clouds started to change. At first it was subtle, but the change picked up momentum fast. The sky was taking on a fiery red hue. Almost as if Marek's blood had infected the storm.

And then the first fat rain drop hit my face. More followed. It was raining, but this was no ordinary downpour. I touched my face and then looked at my hands. They were slick with a sticky, scarlet liquid.

The full horror of what was happening sunk in.

It was raining blood.

17

A drop of rain hit my lips and I tasted copper—real blood was pelting down.

It was painting the world scarlet, soaking the ground and streaking down the jagged mountains of junked cars. Everything was red.

Screaming sirens bashed the air. Four police cruisers were tearing toward the crowd of vampires, flashes of blue in the red downpour. A beat later, the cop cars came to a grinding halt, tires spewing bloody gravel, and spat out unformed officers wielding shotguns and pistols.

Marek's vampires would easily decimate these boys in blue. They were as as good as dead, and there was nothing I could do to save them. I expected Marek's vampires to swarm them like piranhas but to my surprise no such thing happened. The vamps merely watched the phalanx of officers in stony, eerie indifference. Rain pelted their faces, streaking their ragged hoodies crimson. By now, the officers had noticed the strange rainfall, their faces distorting with growing horror.

"Bring up your hands and get on the ground! NOW!"

The officer's voice shook with adrenaline, his shotgun leveled at Marek's undead followers. I had a feeling this was going to get ugly. The cops were on edge, and the moment they started firing, all hell would break loose.

"Officers, stay back!" I yelled, my voice shaky. "You don't know what you're up against here!"

"Shut the fuck up and get on the ground!" one of them shouted. Scarlet rain lashed the officer's face as he turned toward me. He squinted through the veil of blood masking his face. His eyes suddenly went wide. Although I was too far away to see it, I could imagine his pupils turning into pinpoints of red as the blood rain worked its horrific magic. The cop doubled over, racked by violent spasms. His partner spun toward him.

"What's wrong?" the second cop cried out.

The first officer glared up at him, his eyes inhuman, monstrous fangs extending from his mouth. Before his stunned partner could respond, the transformed cop launched into him. With an animalistic shriek, the vampire cop sank his teeth into the other man's neck.

Gunfire went off, followed by terrified screams. This was merely the beginning of the violence to come. More of the officers were changing before my eyes. I watched in gaping horror as the cops became blood-starved monsters, willing to turn on their own partners.

Marek's promise of a vampire apocalypse was becoming a nightmarish reality.

My pulse roared in my ears, fear threatening to overwhelm me. Yet I managed to somehow keep a cool head, willing my mind to a calmer place. Why wasn't the blood rain affecting me in the same way? The only logical explanation I could come up with was that the *Seal of Solomon* was protecting me.

Too bad it wouldn't protect me from vampire fangs or a stray bullet.

Dread crept up my throat at the thought of what might be happening around the Cursed City at this very moment. Was anyone unlucky enough to be outside during the crimson downpour being turned into a blood-hungry monster?

Eying the red clouds above, I saw they were slowly spreading and moving from the outskirts of the city to its bustling center. I had to hope my plan would work before the storm unleashed its wrath on the more densely populated areas. If I failed, the alternative was almost unimaginably horrific.

Marek intended to turn as many of the Cursed City's citizen into vampires as he could, and his new army would prey upon those who escaped the initial effects of the rain. As their numbers swelled, they would shift their focus to other cities. Other countries. An epidemic such as mankind hadn't experienced since the bubonic plague would sweep like wildfire across the globe. Civilization would be washed away in a river of Marek's blood.

With a flash of insight, I understood why Marek had posted the vampire video online. He knew it would get Skulick's attention. It was always about luring me and my partner into his web so he could get his hands on the grail. And now he was offering us front row seats at the end of the world. Talk about the perfect revenge.

Marek's booming voice thrust me out of my fatalistic thoughts. "It has begun! Soon the world of man will give rise to a new order. Mankind will fall. But you, son of Richard, won't be around to see what happens next."

Marek spun toward Archer. "Finish him!"

Archer bounded toward me, a famished attack dog finally freed from her new master's tight leash. She glared at me, lips twisted with hunger, indifferent of our shared past. To the woman I loved, I'd become nothing more than a snack.

I wouldn't use *Hellseeker*. It's what Marek wanted, and I refused to provide him with the satisfaction of seeing me gun down the woman I love. Marek wanted me, the son of his greatest enemy, to die knowing I'd lost everything. Well, I refused to play along and give him the satisfaction.

Especially not if there was still a hope, however slim, of bringing Archer back. My love slammed into me with supernatural force and sent me sprawling. I tried to scramble to my feet, but she was faster.

Eyes blazing with a bottomless thirst, she pinned me down, her fangs an inch from my neck. And that's when the expression on Archer's face changed. The madness lifted. Clarity edged back into her features. For the first time since setting foot in the junkyard, I saw the real Archer staring back at me. She still wasn't human, but neither was she fully vampire anymore. Something fundamental had shifted inside of her.

I glance upward, where Skulick still dangled from the crane. Even from this distance, I recognized the change in him. He'd stopped struggling like a feral beast and was looking around at the scene instead. I had no doubt his razor-sharp intellect was already making sense of the blood-drenched tableau. My partner was back in charge.

"Well, finish him!" Marek bellowed at Archer.

I sensed Marek's growing impatience in his tone. And below that another emotion: confusion. The vampire-demon didn't quite understand why Archer would hesitate in the face of an easy meal.

I gently rolled Archer off of me and helped her stand. She was shaking, and I wrapped an arm around her shoulders. I'd thought I would never get to hold her again, but Archer wasn't a threat to me anymore.

"Raven?" she asked, her voice uncertain.

"It's okay," I murmured. "It's almost over."

One by one, the shrieks died down across the wrecking yard and the transformed vampire cops backed away from each other. The stunned expression plastered across their faces mirrored Archer's reaction. They were slowly waking from a nightmare, awareness creeping back into their shocked gazes.

"What's happening?" Marek demanded to know, his harsh voice cutting the air like barbed wire. The master vampire's confusion was music to my ears.

I whipped out *Hellseeker* from my shoulder holster and leveled it at Marek. I was under no illusion that I could destroy him with my blessed pistol, but that wasn't my intention, at least not yet. For the moment, I had a very different agenda. I wanted to piss the vampire-demon off.

"Looks like your ritual isn't exactly playing out as expected, buddy. I'd say I was sorry, but we both know that's a lie."

Marek's confusion deepened. Despite his monstrous appearance, there was vulnerability in those distorted features now. A note of panic crept into his voice. "What have you done, mortal?"

I remained silent, but the answer was all around him. All of the vampires around us—Skulick, Archer, and the cops, as well as Marek's ragged tribe—were slowly turning back to human. The rain that was supposed to create more vampires was having the exact opposite effect.

The master vampire's giant wings flared out as he

whirled toward me, murder in his animalistic gaze. His reptilian eyes gleamed with naked hatred. How had I turned his ritual against him? Simple, really. Before handing him the cup, I had coated it with angel blood.

What, did you think that with the lives of my friends hanging in the balance, I'd be so foolish as to hand this madman a magical weapon of mass destruction without an ace up my sleeve?

My earlier conversation with Cyon had given me a pretty good idea how Marek intended to use the chalice. Skulick had only managed to procure enough angel blood to cure one vampire, but there was no way in hell I'd choose between him and Archer. I had guessed if the energy generated by the three occult skyscrapers could amplify the power of Marek's blood, the same might hold true for the effects of the angel blood. It had been a gamble, but it was now paying off big time.

I studied Marek, looking for signs that the angel blood's power was working on him, too, but he remained just as ugly as ever. Maybe he'd been a vampire for too many centuries for the curse to be broken. Maybe the demon blood coursing through him counteracted the angelic power. For whatever reason, he remained unaffected—and royally pissed off. While he still didn't grasp how I'd turned the tables on him, he'd figured out who to blame.

A lesser man would have stayed to gloat. But while I

might have successfully thwarted the vampire apocalypse, Marek could still easily tear me apart. The next part of my plan hinged on being able to draw him away from the junkyard.

Marek unleashed a bellowing roar and shot toward me. I unloaded a few rounds into him, which did about as much harm as shooting him with spitballs, while I cut a beeline to my Ducati. None of the former vampires tried to stop me. Though I hated to leave Archer and Skulick behind, they were probably safer here than with me for the time being. Within seconds, I was astride my bike and tearing away into the rainy night. Behind me, I heard Marek taking to the air.

The chase was on.

18

I blasted out of the wrecking yard, the tires of my Ducati devouring the blood-soaked asphalt. Using the angel blood was only the first step of the plan I'd cooked up with Cyon. Now came the tricky part–defeating Marek.

The pounding rain and the Ducati's wailing motor drowned out the beating wings above me. I didn't need to see or hear Marek to know that death was stalking me from above.

As my bike shot down the mostly deserted city streets, I caught sporadic glimpses of homeless people. They stumbled through the mysterious downpour, confused expressions plastered on their faces. Like the cops, the magical rain must've first turned them into vamps and had now changed them back. I predicted that the mother of all hangovers was in store for them as their bodies continued to adjust to all these physical changes. They stared at me with haunted expressions which turned into terror when the spotted the winged monstrosity hurtling after me.

A quick glance at my rear-view mirror confirmed what I already knew. A giant, sleek bat monster loomed above me. Any moment now, Marek would swoop down for the kill.

I cranked up the engine and goosed it. I cut a hard right and braked, waiting. Marek dive-bombed down the side street, my lightning fast maneuver making him overshoot me by a couple of feet. As he crashed into a row of dumpsters, his roar of frustrated rage reverberating among the buildings, I expertly spun the bike around. The Ducati's tires kicked up scarlet water as I shot down the other direction.

Another glimpse at my mirror revealed that Marek was quickly regaining his bearings. Within mere seconds, the vampire-demon was airborne and resumed the chase. I considered pumping a few rounds at the incoming creature, but the weapon's recoil was liable to kick me off my bike.

Stick to the plan, I admonished myself.

My motorcycle screamed down another road, barreled through an empty intersection, and shot into the small park up ahead. The park, like much of the rest of this rundown neighborhood had become a den for druggies and hookers. Let's just say it wasn't a place you wanted to hang out at night—or during daylight hours for that matter. Anyone who'd been outside during the blood rain had cleared out already, no doubt terrified and confused by their recent supernatural ordeal. So much the better for me; I didn't want any innocent bystanders to get caught in what happened next.

My bike growled as I lunged toward the sidewalk. Barely slowing down, I jumped the curb and sped down the narrow stone path that cut through the gloomy park. Darkness wrapped around me like a shroud. Skeletal trees and matted underbrush, now painted red, swayed in the windy downpour as I revved the engine.

I was headed for a small clearing ringed by a copse of barren trees and jagged rocks streaked with graffiti.

I never made it.

The air above me whistled and suddenly I was airborne. For a beat, the now riderless bike continued down the trail before slamming into a blood-streaked park bench.

The dirt path fell away below my flailing legs as Marek lifted me higher, now fifteen feet in the air, his talons painfully digging into my shoulders through my leather biker jacket.

Without thought, I brought up the *Seal of Solomon* and raked it across the vampire's face. There was an inhuman roar of pain, and Marek released me.

My maneuver didn't seem like such a smart move as I

found myself sailing through the air, a scream lodged in my throat. The ground rushed up me at breakneck speed. Luckily, I crashed into the bare branches of a tree instead of planting face-first into the hard ground. The tree slowed my descent enough that the landing rattled every bone in my body instead of shattering them. My helmet and motorcycle jacket absorbed the brunt of the impact, but I was still winded. I laid on the ground for a stunned beat, broken branches raining down on me.

As I struggled to get back to my feet, slipping and sliding on the red grass, I saw my father among the ring of trees. It had to be my mind playing tricks on me. Had to be. The fall must've affected me more severely than first expected. Maybe I had a concussion. Dad urged me to get up. I know I had to be hallucinating, but the surreal vision galvanized me.

Real or not, I wasn't going to let my dad down.

I made it upright and groggily staggered to the center of the park's tiny clearing. I didn't get far before Marek's man-bat form landed in front of me, his leathery wings barring any chance of escape. The master vampire's eye blazed with a terrifying fury.

"*You ruined everything!*" he screamed.

Reacting on pure reflex, I brought up *Hellseeker*. The maneuver made me wince in pain, my bruised ribs reminding me that I'd just survived a fifteen-foot fall in case I'd forgotten. Thank God I hadn't sprained an ankle.

I faced the gargantuan beast, gun held steady. Red rain streamed down Marek's giant wings, making him look like a gargoyle made of blood.

Marek took a menacing step toward me, and the ground shook

"Your father's little toy gun didn't kill me thirty years ago, and it won't be able to stop me today. I'm more powerful than you can imagine."

"Is that so?" I said defiantly. "You've become more than a vampire. You fed on the blood of a demon."

The lack of fear in my voice seemed to give the master vampire pause. But this insight came too late. My eyes caught sight of a new figure in the clearing. It was Cyon, and he was grinning in the bloody rain, his bony visage eerily accentuated by the unnatural downpour.

Marek whirled toward the demon who had been his prisoner. His monstrous gaze ticked from me to Cyon, understanding dawning. For the first time, I detected an undercurrent of fear in Marek's bestial features.

"A monster hunter working with a monster?" Marek asked in disbelief. "Impossible."

"Hello, Marek," Cyon said. "You have taken what wasn't yours. The blood of a demon runs through your veins. My blood."

Cyon took a few steps toward the winged beast, unafraid. This was a creature who had served among Hell's Legions. Confronting a monstrous creature like

Marek didn't faze him. He was a far scarier beast all together.

Cyon continued to advance. "As a demon, there are rules that you now have to obey. Rules that bind our kind. Rules you used against me and which I'm now going to use against you."

Marek found his voice at last. "What are you talking about, demonspawn?"

"Look around you, Marek, and tell me what you see?"

The question hung there for a beat. Marek studied the clearing more carefully. Then he looked down at his clawed feet. His eyes widened as he finally noticed the giant pentagram Cyon and I had drawn on the grass. It was the same one Marek had used to imprison Cyon, albeit much larger. Rocks formed the five points of the star marked with occult glyphs designed to imprison a demon. Cyon had wisely stayed out of the trap.

You guessed it. I'd been the bait to lure Marek into the binding circle from which he could not escape. I'd counted on Marek being so blinded by rage that he wouldn't spot the pentagram until it was too late. Only one last step remained for the trap to spring shut.

I recited a series of words in Latin and Aramaic, drawing on my occult studies, and the pentagram around Marek lit up like a Christmas tree from Hell.

The vampire-demon, still not believing that he could have walked into his own trap, flung himself into the air.

He didn't get far.

After ascending about eight feet, the invisible force field flung him back to the ground with brutal force. Shrieks of frustration burst from his lips as his wings flailed madly. His next tactic was to launch himself at me, but I had stepped out of the pentagram, taking my place next to Cyon. Marek's talons sliced the air and bounced back with violent force when he slammed into the invisible barrier.

There was no escape from the circle. By draining a demon, Marek had gained Cyon's powers—but also his weaknesses.

Cyon stepped up to the edge of the pentagram. The demon's smile sent shivers down my back. The human mask vanished during that moment, and I saw the real monster beneath the earthly disguise. Thank God Skulick didn't know what I'd gotten myself into. He would have chewed me out for even considering a partnership with such an unholy monster.

I spoke slowly with the cadence of a chant. "Marek, you belong to me. You are mine to command. Invoking the power of this binding circle, I cast you down to the pits of Hell where you shall remain for all eternity."

"No! I am immortal! I am—"

Marek's words were cut off as the ground shook and quaked with tremendous force. A giant sinkhole in the shape of a star opened beneath the master vampire, forming a huge cavity in the earth. The walls of the hole began to avalanche in, pulling a suddenly terrified Marek with them. The master vampire struggled to claw his way up through the crumbling dirt. A beat later, he vanished inside the supernatural sink hole, his terrified roar assaulting the night.

Hell was about to welcome its newest inmate.

Couldn't have happened to a nicer vampire-demon hybrid, I thought, kicking a clod of dirt into the hole.

The earth trembled again, and I stumbled forward. A heartbeat later, I found myself tumbling down the supernatural sink hole. I inhaled dirt as I tried to yell for Cyon's help, my hands scrambling, hoping to claw my way up through the crumbling dirt just as Marek had tried.

Cyon loomed above me at the edge of the hungry pit. The demon wordlessly regarded me, his gaze blank, devoid of human feeling. Goddamnit, I knew the demonic bastard was going to double-cross me. I was done for, about to be dragged into Hell. There were a lot of demons who'd be happy to see me.

And then Cyon's hand snapped around my left wrist and pulled me back to the surface. Sweat dripped down my face as I crawled away from the gaping hole. I watched in stunned silence as the earth began to close again, the cavity sealing itself. Moments later, the clearing was back to normal. There were no signs that the ground had ever been dug up or disturbed, the grass pristine. I shook all over as my gaze landed on Cyon.

"You saved me."

"We're even now," the demon said matter-of-factly. "The next time our paths cross…" Cyon's voice trailed off, the threat not needing to be verbalized.

There was a pause between us before the demon vanished in the trees of the park.

Feeling like crap, I slowly stumbled erect. The red downpour had stopped, replaced by a normal shower of rain water. Soon, all traces of the blood ritual would be washed away— but I doubted that would heal all wounds. The memories would persist, especially among those who had been affected by this terrible storm.

Cyon and I had defeated Marek. We had saved the city. Yet all I could think about was Archer and Skulick back at the wrecking yard. I had to get to them and see if they were okay—or at least alive and unharmed. It was probably going to be a pretty long time before either of them was okay again.

I located my bike, its engine still sputtering away next to the bench it had slammed into. Every muscle in my body strained as I up righted the cycle. The front fender was dented from the crash, but overall the damage was minimal. I swung myself onto the bike, and then I was shooting down city roads, on my way back to the wrecking yard that had played such a pivotal part in this latest case.

I was elated to be reunited with Archer and Skulick, but I was worried too. How would Archer cope with the guilt of having taken lives while she was a vampire? How would Skulick react when he found out that I joined forces with a demon? Worse, what would he say when I told him that I'd let Cyon walk away?

The demon was still out there. Weakened and trapped in our world, but also representing an unknown variable. Would he continue to oppose his master, or would he become my newest enemy in the hopes of getting back in Morgal's good graces? Only time would tell. One thing was for certain: Our paths were bound to cross again.

My heart beating faster, I pushed the throttle as far as it would go.

I would face the next threat, whatever it turned out to be, but I wouldn't be facing it alone. I tore into the wrecking yard, ready to be reunited with the two people who mattered the most to me in the whole world.

THE END

Raven and Skulick will return in DEMON DAWN.

GRAB IT HERE.

US: Shadow Detective 4: Demon Dawn

UK: Shadow Detective 4: Demon Dawn

MORE BOOKS ARE COMING SOON. Visit amazon.com/author/williammassa and press "**FOLLOW**" to be automatically notified of future releases.

The best is yet to come.

Want to get an email when the next SHADOW DETECTIVE title is released and receive a free novella? Subscribe to my newsletter!
Click here to get started: **http://eepurl.com/Ki8QH**

Thank you for reading. Please consider leaving a review if you enjoyed the book. Even a short review will be super-helpful and allow other readers to discover the series. For your convenience, I have include this direct link:

http://www.amazon.com/review/create-review/ref+cm_cr_dp_wrt_btm?ie=UTF8&asin=B071YX2N48

Please enjoy this special preview of DEMON DAWN.

THE TIRES of my Equus Bass screeched to a halt as I pulled

up to the imposing stone steps of the Museum of World History. Gothic arches and other majestic architectural flourishes were designed to awe visitors. Even someone as cynical as me couldn't avoid feeling a little impressed.

I parked my car and got out. As I approached the structure on foot, I barely registered the banners announcing an upcoming Egyptian Exhibit. There were glimpses of eerie mummies, pyramids and ornately decorated sarcophagi. I used to be a sucker for that stuff until I faced my first crazed mummy back in Cairo. My job sure can suck the joy out of childhood fantasies.

The area in front of the museum resembled a warzone. Everywhere I looked I saw police cruisers, flashing sirens, armed SWAT teams and tight-lipped officers with their firearms drawn. This crowd hadn't gathered here today to take advantage of some group discount; something bad was going down. The fact that Detective Benson had contacted me less than thirty minutes ago with an order to get my ass down here was my first clue that the threat was of a supernatural nature. The second clue was the mark of Morgal, the scar the arch-demon had branded me with when I was but a child, which flared up the moment I stepped out of the car.

Dark forces were at work, that much was certain. And judging by the armed SWAT presence, this wasn't a mere occult murder scene. A force not of this world was still active within the museum.

My eyes searched the crowd, and I zeroed in on the tall African-American detective who was my liaison with the force. About a year earlier, an apocalyptic cult had tried to tear a hole between our world and the dimension of darkness in this very city. My mentor Skulick and I had interrupted the Crimson's Circle infernal ritual, saving the city from a demonic invasion. But our victory had been bittersweet at best—the cult's black magic ceremony had weakened the barrier between the two worlds. Ever since that fateful day, this place had become a hotbed for supernatural activity. In other words, poor Detective Benson had seen some crazy shit since Skulick and I showed up in his town.

For that reason—and many others—the law shared a love-and-hate relationship with yours truly. The authorities both appreciated my help and resented that I was needed in the first place. Hey, I couldn't blame them. Paranormal trouble seemed to follow me like a shadow, infecting not just me but the people I cared about as well. Nevertheless, Benson seemed to have warmed up to me lately. He'd never admit this to my face, but I think he was beginning to realize that I was here to help. I wasn't part of the problem but part of the solution. Just like the armed men around me, I spent my days and nights keeping this city safe from the nightmares that threatened its citizens.

I sidled up to Benson, who was barking orders at his

men. A group of cops fell in step with the SWAT team, the armed men preparing for a direct assault of the museum.

"Just another night on the job, huh?"

Benson's steely gaze landed on me, devoid of any humor. Maybe I'd overestimated how much the man had warmed up to me.

"You're late," he growled. "My boys are just about to go in."

"Care to fill me in on what we're up against here?"

Benson turned away from his men and led me to a mobile command center. A group of officers were hunched over flickering monitors and other computer equipment. Benson nodded at one of the techies, and the man pulled up a video on his screen. The main exhibit floor of the museum appeared, filled with Egyptian cultural artifacts. Ornate burial urns, stone masks, and statues of mythological figures abounded.

My gaze ticked from the jackal-headed god Anubis to the large, highly adorned golden sarcophagus at the center of the exhibit floor. A crowd of museum visitors was milling around the ancient coffin. The angles of the scene kept changing, the footage apparently courtesy of the museum's many security cams.

Suddenly, a group of armed men filled the display area. The audio kicked in, and I heard the phalanx of men barking orders at the crowd in accented English. The language sounded a lot like Arabic. Over the years, I'd traveled the globe hunting monsters with Skulick, and I'd picked up snippets of almost every language. Chasing demons and ghosts across the planet sure as hell beat your average college degree.

"About an hour ago, a group of terrorists attacked the museum," Benson explained. "And that's when things started to get really weird."

On-screen, the terrorists opened fire at the ceiling. Visitors screamed and ran for their lives. One of the armed intruders, a bald, goatee-wearing individual whose eyes shone with a fanatical glee, broke open a nearby display case and removed a ceremonial dagger. He stepped up to the ancient coffin and began to chant in a language that definitely wasn't Arabic.

A chill shot up my spine. Occult rituals can have that effect on me nowadays. Chanting is always a precursor to the real horror.

The terrorist leader cut a deep gash into the palm of his outstretched hand with the ceremonial dagger. Blood drizzled onto the coffin and the lid began to vibrate. I clenched my teeth, unable to look away. What horror were these fanatics unleashing upon the world? I was afraid I already knew—and I was not in the mood to deal with another mummy.

A heartbeat later, the lid slid open and a bandaged arm exploded from the golden coffin. A figure dragged itself from the sarcophagus, a mummified horror from another age. Screams filled the museum as the image onscreen started to break up, lines of static multiplying across the screen.

The terrorist leader kept chanting despite the mounting horror in his voice. Fanatical fool. Then a bestial roar drowned out all other sounds. Something ancient and monstrous had been awoken from its long slumber. Bursts of staccato gunfire followed, and then the screaming began in earnest.

The screen went dark.

Benson gave me a long look, his mouth etched into a grim line. "Less than an hour ago, all security cams inside the museum went offline. No one has left the building since. We don't know how many people are still alive in there. Ten minutes ago, we sent in our first SWAT team. We lost contact with them almost immediately. Whatever horror these fanatics unleashed, it's still in there. And it managed to take out a whole team of highly trained men."

I considered Benson's words as I studied the team ready to follow their lost brothers into battle—they were little more than sacrificial lambs headed for the slaughter. I doubted they would fare much better against Egyptian black magic than the first team.

"Any idea whose sarcophagus was on display in there?" I asked. Information was power in any conflict. The sooner I understood who—or rather what—we were up against, the sooner I could figure out a way to stop it.

Benson looked down at a notepad. "The pharaoh Khafer Namer from the Early Dynastic period. Rumored to have dabbled in sorcery and black magic rituals, according to the museum press kit. They were playing up the black magic angle to bring visitors to the exhibit."

I shook my head. That sure had backfired. The museum's attempt to sell tickets had caught the attention of the wrong group of fanatics.

"The name mean anything to you?" Benson asked.

I shook my head. Truth be told, not really. Since my Cairo adventure, I had stayed clear of Egyptian magic. I didn't quite know what I was up against here but past experiences had proven that both my blessed pistol *Hellseeker,* which had been forged from a holy sword, and my protective magical ring, *the Seal of Solomon,* could be quite effective against nightmares from a variety of pantheons. I had also brought my silver dagger along. Armed with these three weapons, I felt ready to face the horrors waiting for me within the museum.

"I'm going in alone," I said.

"SWAT has been chomping at the bit to do their thing. They don't leave their men behind."

Their men are dead, I thought fatalistically but kept my mouth shut.

I couldn't blame the officers impatiently eying the museum. Their brothers in arms were inside, but they were stuck out here. No matter how brave they were, their armor and weapons would barely slow down the creature the Egyptian terrorists had unleashed. Luckily, what I lacked in overall firepower, I made up for with occult knowledge and magical weaponry.

"How much time can you give me?" I asked.

Benson exchanged a quick glance with the SWAT commander before shifting his attention back to me. "You have ten minutes."

Ten minutes to face down an ancient Egyptian monster that had most likely destroyed a whole SWAT team. Piece of cake.

I turned away from the armed team. They watched in what I liked to think was impressed silence as I made my way to the museum's main entrance. I felt their stares, sensed their begrudging respect. Perhaps they didn't quite know what to make of the bearded, trench coat wearing, slightly rumpled occult expert, but it takes a certain amount of courage to walk into the dark places of the world when you know monsters are waiting inside. Me and the boys in blue had that in common.

Soon I was navigating the labyrinthine exhibit halls of the museum. The building, as much as the ancient artifacts it housed, conveyed a sense of history. I could feel the weight of the centuries at my back as I explored the dimly lit space. The past was alive within these walls.

Literally.

I hurried through the first chamber, past the creepy

Egyptian artifacts. The beast-headed statues cast grotesquely distorted shadows, the ancient artwork's dark power palpable. My footsteps rang hollowly as I picked up my pace.

I stumbled upon the first body in the next room. The downed SWAT officer's lifeless, bulging eyes stared blankly into mine, his MP5 machine pistol cast aside. Bullets pockmarked the walls, and several priceless artifacts had been damaged beyond repair.

As I edged deeper into the darkness, more bodies followed. I kneeled before one of the corpses, my guard up. Deep bluish marks had discolored the skin around the dead man's neck. Almost as if he he'd been strangled to death. Several other bodies showed similar wounds. There were no other signs of violence, no blood.

My gaze combed the museum floor. Moonlight seeped through a large skylight overhead, painting a lattice of flickering shadows across the exhibit. It was designed to recreate an ancient embalming chamber, with a long gruesome hook, canopic jars, and other tools for making mummies laid out as if waiting to be used. The mummified remains of the long dead peered out from display cases and open coffins.

I didn't blame the museum for capitalizing on the macabre. Mummies sold tickets. Unfortunately, there were fresh corpses scattered throughout the exhibit, and one of the mummies was walking around in search of more victims. It wouldn't hesitate to add me to the grisly collection of the dead in this room.

I was thrust out of dark musings as something stirred in the far corner of the room. A shadow flared across the wall, moving too quickly for me to see what it was. My eyes darted from side to side, searching. I heard a noise that might have been the sound of bandage-wrapped bones moving in the darkness—or it might have been my imagination.

Get a grip, Raven, I told myself.

And then all hell broke loose.

ABOUT THE AUTHOR

William Massa is a produced screenwriter and bestselling Amazon author. His film credits include *Return to House on Haunted Hill* and he has sold pitches and scripts to Warner, USA TV, Silver Pictures, Dark Castle, Maverick and Sony.

William has lived in New York, Florida, Europe and now resides in Venice Beach surrounded by skaters and surfers. He writes science fiction and dark fantasy/urban fantasy horror with an action-adventure flavor.

Writing can be a solitary pursuit but rewriting can be a group effort. I strive to make each book better than the last and feedback is incredibly helpful. If you have notes, thoughts or comments about this book or want to contact me, feel free to contact me at:

williammassabooks@gmail.com

ALSO BY WILLIAM MASSA

THE SHADOW DETECTIVE SERIES

Cursed City

Soul Catcher

Blood Rain

Demon Dawn

Skull Master

Ghoul Night

Witch Wars

Crimson Circle

Hell Breaker

THE OCCULT ASSASSIN SERIES

Damnation Code

Apocalypse Soldier

Spirit Breaker

Soul Jacker

THE GARGOYLE KNIGHT SERIES

Gargoyle Knight

Gargoyle Quest

STAND ALONES

Fear the Light

Printed in Great Britain
by Amazon